Tales Fabulous and Fairy

Volume 1

# Also by Kim Antieau

**Novels**
*The Blue Tail • Broken Moon • Butch*
*Church of the Old Mermaids • Coyote Cowgirl • Deathmark*
*The Desert Siren • The Fish Wife • Her Frozen Wild*
*The Gaia Websters • Jewelweed Station*
*The Jigsaw Woman • Maternal Instincts • Mercy, Unbound*
*Queendom: Feast of the Saints • The Rift • Ruby's Imagine*
*Swans in Winter • Whackadoodle Times • Whackadoodle Times Two*

**Nonfiction**
*Answering the Creative Call*
*Certified: Learning to Repair Myself and the World*
*in the Emerald City*
*Counting on Wildflowers: An Entanglement*
*Old Mermaids Book of Days and Nights • The Old Mermaids Oracle*
*The Salmon Mysteries:*
*a Reimagining of the Eleusinian Mysteries*
*The Salmon Mysteries Workbook:*
*Reimagining the Eleusinian Mysteries*
*Under the Tucson Moon*

**Collections**
*Entangled Realities* (with Mario Milosevic)
*The First Book of Old Mermaids Tales*
*Trudging to Eden*

**Chapbook**
*Blossoms*

**Blog**
*www.kimantieau.com*

**Photography**
*www.kimantieau.smugmug.com*

# Tales
## Fabulous and Fairy
### Volume I

# Kim Antieau

Tales Fabulous and Fairy, Volume 1
by Kim Antieau



ISBN: 978-1-949644-37-1



Original publication of these stories as follows:
"Foundling," *Daughters of Nyx,* Spring 1994
"Seeing Pink," Green Snake Publishing, 2011
"Briar Rose," *Metahorror,* 1992
"Dragon Pearl," *Furious Spinner,* 2003
"Rose Red and Snow White," *Journal of Mythic Arts,* Winter 2002
"The Señorita and the Cactus Thorn," *Coyote Road,* 2007
"A Strange Attractor," *Counting on Wildflowers,* 2005

Cover photo by Kim Antieau
showing a detail from a tree mural by Terri Windling.

Book design by Mario Milosevic and Kim Antieau.
Special thanks to Nancy Milosevic.



Electronic editions of this book
are available at most e-book stores.

Published by Green Snake Publishing
www.greensnakepublishing.com

www.kimantieau.com

For Dennis Etchison

# Contents

# The Foundling

In the time before the dam, on the day his wife died, Richard stumbled into the jungle he hated. He had to get away from his daughter's whimpering, her cries like those of some unknown bird living in the forest beyond the banks of the Tocantins River. The day they finished the dam could not come soon enough for him: Then they would flood the rainforest. The jungle. The place where the beasts played and the cries of children turned into butterfly songs. He had brought his wife here, to this place he hated, and she had died. Yet he fell into the jungle to flee the cries of his daughter.

The forest blurred through his tears. The noises, smells,

and touch of things against his skin startled him. He tried to fall back out again, into the civilization he was trying to build on the banks of that Brazilian river, but he could not find his way out. Suddenly, he heard the cries of another child. Or the screams of a monkey? He followed the sound until he reached a clump of ferns. He leaned over and found a naked baby boy supported just above the ground by the soft green fingers of the ferns.

Without thinking, he took the baby from the ferns and held him up. Bubbles popped from the baby's lips as he smiled. Off to his side, Richard glimpsed movement. He turned from the boy. Was that a woman resting against a nearby tree, her chin on her chest, her hand touching the smooth black tree trunk? Richard blinked. No, only a shadow passing by or the sun trying to find a hole in the canopy.

"Something for my Lena," he said, holding the boy above his head. "To keep her company." And then he walked away from the ferns and the shadow woman by the tree and found his way out of the forest and into the house where his wife had died.

Richard put the boy in the crib with his daughter, Lena. She stopped crying and stared at the brown baby next to her. Then she laughed and reached her tiny fingers out to touch his hand. Richard went back to work, away from the forest, to forget his wife, and left Lena with the boy and the woman Katy from Tucurui.

The boy, who was called Cauffee by Richard because he was brown, and the girl, Lena, who was as white as the inside of a coconut, grew together and loved each other very much. When Richard wasn't looking, they went into the forest together and became shadows. They listened to the sighs of the cats and mimicked the monkeys overhead. Sometimes they slithered across low branches hissing like snakes. They were children of the forest even as Richard helped build the dam to destroy it.

And Richard hardly noticed as his daughter grew taller and more like his dead wife. When the dam was finished, he watched the forest die as the water poured over it. The stench of death filled his wife's house. The children cried. Richard took them and Katy to the next place along the river, and Lena and Cauffee laughed, quietly, because they had the forest once again. During the day, Richard went to his offices at Eletronorte Brazil to build another dam.

One day, Lena and Cauffee walked along the banks of the river holding hands, and Lena said, "I will never ever leave you."

"And I will never leave you," Cauffee said. He leaned down until his lips touched hers.

Lena smiled as the air dried his kiss from her mouth.

Katy saw the kiss and was disturbed. Though she loved both children, she believed Cauffee should live in the forest with his own people. Later she told Richard about the kiss.

"Cauffee cannot live here any longer," Richard said to Lena. He stood by the mantel where no fireplace had ever been built. He straightened his tie and smiled at his pretty daughter. Someday he would be rid of this jungle, and he would take her home where everything was not so close to the earth. Lena sat on the floor. The white dress she wore was pulled up around her legs as she moved the pieces of some game around on the floor.

"What do you mean 'away'?" Lena asked. "This is his home."

"He is not one of us," Richard said. "He should be with his own people."

"Who are my people?" Cauffee stood in the entrance to the living room.

Richard wondered when Cauffee had gotten so tall. He was no longer a boy.

"You could work on the dam," Richard said. "I can find you a job. I should have done it long ago. But you've always been such a comfort to Lena. You aren't really children any longer, however. You, Cauffee, are part of the jungle. Lena is not."

Cauffee and Lena glanced at each other. They spoke to each other without words. It had never bothered Richard before, but it did now. They had created a world of their own, and he had only just noticed he didn't belong.

And this boy—man?—had kissed his daughter. He had seen him kiss her before. A child kissing a child. It was different now. Cauffee was a man from the jungle. Maybe it was calling to him. The jungle. It had taken Richard's wife. Given her some kind of fever that modern science could not cure.

Lena looked at her father. "I will never leave him."

Richard laughed. "You are a child," he said. "You don't

know what you'll never do. I said I would never come to this place and I did. Then I said I would never stay, and here I am." Lena stared at him. "Well," he said, shrugging. "We will speak of this later."

He started to leave the house and then stopped and came back to the living room where Cauffee and Lena now sat together on the floor, their heads close, speaking without talking. "I don't want you in the jungle, Lena. It's too dangerous."

After Richard left them, Lena and Cauffee went outside and into the jungle, away from the manicured play town that Eletronorte had created for the workers while the dam was being built. They ran until they reached a patch of moss and there they lay.

"I have loved you since I first saw you," Lena said. "You are in my heart and mind. I will never leave you."

"And I have loved you even before your father took me from my mother," he said. He kissed her lips.

Then, as they often did in the forest, they took off their clothes and let the air and moss stroke their bodies. This time, they pressed their skins against each other. As they twined themselves around one another, the cats breathed in their sighs and the monkeys talked quietly in the trees.

Katy had seen Cauffee and Lena go into the forest. She ran after Richard and brought him home. Richard called to several men to follow him, and he stepped into the jungle again for the first time since he had brought Cauffee out of it. The shadows slid across his body. They made him dizzy.

Cauffee and Lena heard the men approaching.

"I'll never forsake you," Lena said.

"Nor I you," Cauffee said. And they moved closer together.

"Then you must become a snake and I the butterfly on your forehead," Lena said.

Richard called out to his daughter, and the jungle answered him. The snake slipped up a tree while a white butterfly rested on his back. Some beast roared from within the forest. Richard felt his heart race and his blood pound. What was Cauffee doing with his daughter? How could he have been so stupid, bringing the beast out of the jungle? Into his home.

Richard turned from the snake and butterfly and followed the men out of the jungle. He waited for the pair at his house. When the men had gone, Cauffee moved inside Lena, and she in him, touching his heart with her butterfly wings.

Lena's father made Cauffee move to the village. Cauffee did not understand the people there, and he cried for Lena. She whimpered, too, reminding Richard of the day his wife died. He looked out into the night and listened to the jungle noises. Soon the forest would be gone. Then he and Lena would leave.

"Daddy?" Lena stood in the doorway, her eyes wet with tears. She looked so much like his wife. Her voice. Skin. His wife had had skin so white. Like linen that had never been worn. Touched. Then the jungle had touched her.

Killed her.

Lena picked a leaf out of her hair and said, "I thought he was like a son to you."

"He cannot be my son any longer, Lena," Richard said. "You are a child still. You don't understand. He is different from us."

"Being away from him is like having my heart torn in half, Daddy," she said. "I love you, but I cannot live without my heart."

Richard thought of Cauffee's hand on Lena's white skin. He looked out at the dark. "I hate it here," he said. "I don't know why I stayed." He looked back at his daughter. "He cannot have you."

Lena went to her room again and listened to Cauffee's cries brought to her by the other forest animals. In the morning, after Richard had gone to work, Lena dropped a white powder into Katy's coffee and waited for the woman to fall to sleep. Then she ran into the jungle. She ran until one of the shadows moved away from the trees to run with her.

"I will never forsake you," Lena said.

Cauffee stopped and took her into his arms, kissed her forehead, and said, "Nor I you."

They walked until they tired, and then the trees closed about them while they slept and opened when they made love. The birds dropped berries into their laps for them to eat. Near nightfall, they heard the sound of men. Lena's father called for her. He was crying. No, the forest had changed the sound. He was screaming.

"We will never forsake each other," Lena said. "You must become like a bush, and I will become your flower."

The shadows slipped around them, and it was almost dark when Richard came upon the bush with one pink flower growing from it like a beacon.

"My God," he said. "It's dark and I'm going to be here alone in this jungle." He sat next to the bush and began to cry. "I will be left alone, without my wife or daughter. Both taken by the jungle." The two men with him pointed into the grayness.

"There's a place just beyond where we can stay," one said. "We won't be alone."

Richard shook his head—they didn't understand—and then he left the bush and flower behind as he followed the men further into the jungle.

He slept apart from the others, the jungle noises in his ears, creeping into his blood, and he dreamed of Lena, her skin like the feathers on a swan, her dress falling from her until she was standing naked, holding her arms out to him.

He awakened to blackness and cursed the jungle for his dream. He would find his daughter and take her from this place. When he slept again, he dreamed of the snake and the butterfly. The shadows slipped away until the snake became the bush and the butterfly the pink flower.

As dawn came and her father slept, Lena lay next to Cauffee and felt him stir against her, coming alive, awake, moving into her, kissing her face and breast. She laughed and the forest echoed her laugh and stroked her bare back.

"I will never forsake you," she said.

"Nor I you," he said.

Richard awakened suddenly. *The bush and the flower.* He moved quickly through the forest, knowing it now as he had not known it before. He thought of his dead wife and the shadow woman who had slept while he took her child. Or had the woman been a part of his imagination? Maybe Cauffee was part of his imagination, too. Perhaps all of the jungle—the world, this day—was part of his imagination.

They heard him coming.

Richard stopped where he knew the bush had been. In its place was a small pond with a tiny white bird swimming on it.

He knelt by the edge of the pond. "You can't have her," he said. "I will quench my thirst with you." He put his lips on the water. The bird flew up and away and then Cauffee was next to Richard, his hands on his hips, his legs spread apart.

"You will destroy your own daughter," Cauffee said.

Richard wiped his hand across his lips and drops of water fell into the pond. "I only want her back," he said.

"We will never leave each other," Cauffee said, "or this jungle."

"But I will drown it," Richard said, "and you will die if you stay."

"We will find another place," Cauffee answered.

"You cannot have her," Richard said, and he looked

within himself, where the jungle beat, where it had always been, and he found the brightly colored shadows of himself. He dove toward the pond, a small silver fish now, his gills shining like rainbows in the dappled sunlight.

A dragonfly kissed the surface of the water that became Lena again. She smiled and took Cauffee's hand. Where the pond had been, the fish twitched on the wet dirt.

"He doesn't know how to come back," Cauffee said.

Lena picked up the fish and began running, flying across the canopy with the monkeys and insects. The birds carried her part way, the butterflies the rest of the way. The fish flapped against Lena's skin. Then, before her father died, Lena reached the dam of her childhood and dropped him into the reservoir. The fish slipped through the scum, became a flash of light in Lena's eyes, and then was gone.

"I will never forsake you," Lena said when she was by Cauffee's side again.

"Nor I you," Cauffee said.

They held hands and walked deep into the forest. There they lived happily together for many years, becoming shadows and whispers other people mistook for snakes or butterflies or the sighs of cats.

♦♦♦

The tales in this collection are not all straight retellings of fairy tales and folk tales, but they all have their genesis in myths, fairy tales, and folk tales. This one was inspired by Grimm's "The Foundling." In it, a forester finds a little boy in a tree and brings him back to be a companion to his daughter, Lena. The children love each other deeply, instantly, and promise never to forsake one another. In the original tale, when the children try to escape an evil cook, they change themselves into a rose-bush and a rose, a church and a chandelier, a pond and a duck swimming in it to hide. They end up drowning the cook and then safely returning home again.

I set it in the Brazilian jungle after I re-read Catherine Caufield's amazing book *In the Rainforest*. She vividly describes the destruction of the rainforest in order to build a dam. Each time I read the book, I wonder what magic and wonder has been lost for the sake of modernity.

# Seeing Pink

Mata dangled her fingers in the lukewarm water that flowed beneath her grandmother's wooden houseboat. A scarlet dragonfly flew close to Mata's face, probably eyeing an errant insect in the white orchid Mata had stuck in her hair after snatching it from the river as it floated by. The water close to Mata quivered, and her heartbeat quickened as it always did when the pink dolphins neared. She knew she should take her hand out of the Solimões—the great Amazon river—before something took her hand off, but she remained as still as the half-moon hanging in the pale blue sky above her head like the half-shuttered eye of a lizard.

The water was sunset pink now. Bubbles floated up amidst the pink, like the fizz on the champagne her uncle Jaco had brought home after his divorce last year.

The champagne had been pink, too, when she and her uncle stood outside under a sky red with dusk-drenched clouds.

"I like the way the sun colors the clouds," Mata told her uncle while they tried to finish the champagne before her grandmother found out.

Jaco made a noise. "That's not the sun. That's the reflection of the botos—the Encantados. They mostly come out at dusk and dawn, you know. That's when they lure us poor innocents to their enchanted city."

Mata laughed. "You sound like Grandma. Besides, I heard you jumped right in. No one had to lure you."

He grinned and upended the bottle. Then he said, "Yes, that's true, because the kiss of a boto woman is sweeter than any champagne."

"Hah!" Grandmother came out to stand beside them. "You and your brother have empty heads when it comes to the botos."

Mata looked at her grandmother, waiting to hear more about her father, but Grandmother glanced at her, then snatched the bottle from Uncle Jaco. "Did you leave any for your poor mother? And Mata is too young for champagne or stories of kisses."

Grandmother walked back inside the open houseboat, swinging the bottle at her side.

"She thinks you're still twelve, you know," Jaco said.

Mata shook her head, "No, she thinks I'm five. If she ever figures out I'll be eighteen next year I think she'll have a heart attack."

Now Mata waited for the pink dolphins to break the surface of the water. Suddenly the dragonfly flitted away, the water was dark again, and Grandmother was standing over her.

"Mata! I need your help with dinner. How many times have I told you to keep your fingers out of the river? Why become food for the opportune?"

Mata pushed herself up and laughed. She put her arm across her grandmother's shoulders.

"I was waiting for the botos," Mata said.

"I would rather you were eaten by fish than taken by an Encantado. At least your life would have some use if you were fish food!"

Mata had asked her grandmother many times why she hated the pink dolphins.

"They're unnatural," Grandmother always said, "and evil."

When Mata asked Ramon Perez, the shaman, about the dolphins, he told her, "Your grandma is not part of this place the way your grandfather was. She moved here to be with him. Then he died, and she was left alone. She doesn't understand that the Encantados are sacred to us. They can be ridiculous, awesome, terrifying, and heal-ing. Your grandmother sees the world in black and white, you understand? No pink. But you—you are a child of the river. You are dolphin-kissed. Dolphin-blessed. When your grandmother can see pink, then maybe she will have a home here."

Mata went into the houseboat to help her grandmother prepare dinner for the new research team that had arrived earlier in the day. Grandmother seemed nervous, which surprised Mata. The research house had been tethered next to their house for as long as Mata could remember, and the scientists and tourists came with the rains every year.

Mata tried to joke with her grandmother as they cut up fruit and cooked the fish. Mata liked this time of the year. It was as if the river was becoming herself again, spreading into the rainforest, the fish following eagerly and then waiting for fruit to drop from the trees into their open mouths. When Mata was younger, she wondered if the people in the Encante—the enchanted dolphin city— walked around with baskets to gather any of the falling, drifting fruit the fish had missed.

"And where does the Encante go when the river recedes each year?" Mata asked her grandmother as she breaded a fillet. It was a question she had asked every year since she was little.

"Into your dreams," Grandmother said, "into the dreams you have in the morning hours, so don't sleep in too late. It's then the lazy get caught by the botos."

Mata smiled. "Grandmother, why are you nervous about the scientists? They're just like the ones who come every year."

"What?" She looked at her granddaughter. "I'm not nervous about them."

"Then what?"

"Nothing. Just strange noises in the night lately have been keeping me up. The scientists don't bother me. No. Who cares about them?"

The researchers were usually white and English-speaking. For the most part, they ignored Mata and her family, except to say things like, "I don't eat fish. Sorry." "How was this cooked? I don't eat deep-fried anything." "What kind of fish is this? It has teeth." Mata spoke English and Portuguese, so she sometimes translated conversations between scientists or took some of them out in the boat. She did not socialize with them—or have any desire to socialize with them. They all seemed a bit strange to her. She didn't imagine these new researchers would be any different.

Uncle Jaco came into the house, and the three of them piled pieces of pirarucu, avocados, melons, and limes on plates, then put the plates on a tray. Jaco carried the tray in the air as he walked across the plank that linked the two houses. Mata followed.

They walked around to the other side of the house where five white men and two white women sat gazing into the river while swiping insects off their arms.

"Ah, food!" Margaret said as they set the tray on a rickety folding table. Margaret came to the station nearly every year. "Hello, Jaco, Mata. Can I help?"

Margaret introduced the new scientists to Jaco and Mata. Most of them only half-listened to her as they headed for the food—except for a young blond American named Dennis.

"Nice to meet you," he said. "Mata. That's an unusual name. What's it mean?"

Mata shrugged. She was suddenly—and uncharacteristically—tongue-tied.

"What a question," the other woman said. (Diana?) She got a plate of food, then returned to her chair. "Do you know what your name means?"

The blond man turned away from Mata, and she took the empty tray from her uncle and quickly left as the blond man responded.

"Actually I do know what my name means," he said. "It's from Dionysus. The Greek god of wine."

Mata heard several people giggle. She quickly walked across the board to her house again. Her heart was racing, her hands were tingling.

"What's wrong with you?" her grandmother asked. "You're flushed."

"I'm fine," Mata said as she stepped away from her grandmother's heat-seeking hand.

Thunder awakened Mata. Lightning split the night sky, momentarily letting in daylight before sealing up the cracks again. Rain clattered on the roof. Mata listened to the familiar creak of her hammock—and Grandmother's and Uncle Jaco's. She looked out at the flooded forest.

Lightning flashed again, and in that instant Mata saw a naked white woman floating above the water. All white. Even her hair was light-colored. She slowly raised her left arm. Her fingers moved toward herself, then toward Mata, as if beckoning Mata to her. And she grinned—a lopsided grin, kind of like Uncle Jaco's smile when he was drunk. Suddenly, the woman's feet and legs became a tail, and the rest of her body melted into something else and slipped into the water.

Mata gasped. The instant ended. The world darkened.

"It is nobody," Grandmother whispered from her hammock. "It is nothing." Just as she used to when Mata was a child.

Mata blinked, then closed her eyes and went to sleep.

At breakfast, Mata helped serve the researchers. Dennis grinned at her as he ate. Mata was struck speechless again and hurried away. Later Dennis went out in a boat with Uncle Jaco to look for botos. Mata watched them leave and wished she were going with them. She wanted to sit beside the blond man. She liked his smell—and his blue eyes. They were like those photographs she had seen of the Earth from space.

Dennis waved to her, smiling as though they were old friends. She hesitated, then waved, too.

"What made you afraid last night?" her grandmother asked, coming up beside her.

"I saw a woman floating above the water," Mata said. "An Encantado, I think, only she wasn't wearing a hat. You said you could spot boto-people because they wore hats to cover the blow hole."

"Not always," Grandmother said. Mata could tell from her voice that her grandmother had seen the woman, too.

"You stay away from her. What about that boy? The one with Jaco. You like him?"

Mata shrugged.

"He seems like a nice boy. It's time you started thinking of leaving here."

Leaving here? This was her home. She was never leaving here. "You want me to leave? And with this Dennis person? You don't know anything about him. Maybe *you* should think about leaving here. You're the one who has never felt at home."

"It's true," Grandmother said. "I do not understand what the birds say, or the river, or the trees. Or even the people. I don't know why I stay."

"You don't understand because you don't try to understand," Mata said. "It's always been alien to you. For me, it's home."

Grandmother shook her head. "No, you are young. You should leave this place."

"You've been sorry that you left your home, Grandma. Why do you want me to leave mine?"

"You could go live with your father."

"And where would that be?" Mata asked. "I've seen him a dozen times in eighteen years."

"I know where he is," Grandmother said, turning to go back into the house. "Don't be so hard on him. He never got over your poor sainted mother's death."

Mata sighed. Her grandmother never said her mother's name. She only ever referred to her as "your poor sainted mother."

"You are not going to get rid of me that easily, Grandma."

Jaco and Dennis returned a few hours later. Dennis sat in their house and drank beer with Grandmother and Jaco. Mata did not like to drink. It made her sick and dizzy. It was too hot and muggy to do anything else, however, so she sat with the three of them.

"We didn't see a single boto," Dennis said. "We saw several of the other dolphins, but no pink ones. I heard Mata attracts botos whenever she's out on the river."

"Who told you that?" Grandmother asked, glaring at her son.

"Margaret," Dennis said.

Jaco smiled at his mother.

"Those aren't dolphins following her," Grandmother said. "They're piranhas. They go after anyone. You watch out now. Don't get into that water. They'll eat you up."

"They're not piranhas," Mata said, finally able to speak in front of the blond man. "The botos have always liked me."

"I can't take Dennis out later," Jaco said. "I'm helping Margaret with the generator. Maybe Mata could go out with him instead."

Mata waited respectfully for her grandmother's response.

"Don't let him fall into the Solimões," Grandmother finally said. "You know the piranhas prefer blonds."

The motor putt-putted as the small boat made tiny wakes through the still water. Mata steered the boat around the partially submerged trees. She preferred rowing through the forest to walking through it when the flood waters receded. These times always felt magical, precious. She was experiencing the world as few others got to.

She and Dennis gazed out at the water-logged forest they floated through. Epithytes hung from branches like frayed green blankets someone had discarded. Two blue, yellow, and green macaws sat side by side in one of the trees, blinking as they watched the humans go by. Nearby, several spider monkeys jumped from branch to branch, as though trying to keep the boat in sight.

"Do you like ferrying around people like me?" Dennis asked.

"I don't mind," she said. "It's good money."

"I bet a lot of the foreigners coming down here are very condescending to you and your family."

"What's that mean?" Mata asked.

Dennis looked at her, and she grinned.

"Oh, you got me," Dennis said. "I guess I was being a bit condescending myself."

"I don't really pay much attention to how they treat me," she said. "But I remember one woman. She said to me, 'All your fish have such big teeth.' Then she went on to explain that our fish have these big teeth to crack the seeds from fruit that falls into the river. As if I didn't know that! It was funny because then I said, 'Yes, many fish don't eat at all when the forest isn't flooded.' She was so surprised that I could know anything about the place where I live."

Dennis laughed. "I imagine she didn't make that mistake again."

Mata maneuvered the boat into a kind of clearing. She shut off the motor, and the boat drifted slightly.

"Are they here?" Dennis asked.

"Shhh," she said.

They waited quietly, staring at the water. Then suddenly the water became lighter in color, heavier in density. Something changed that Mata couldn't quite put into words. Suddenly pink and red and mottled fins broke the surface all around them. Mata heard, "Schhhaaaaaa! Chaaaaaa!" as several botos exhaled, then swam around the boat.

Without thinking, Mata put her hand out over the boat. She laughed. Two dozen or more pink dolphins surrounded them. Two leaped up, and she looked into their small eyes as they turned their heads from side to side. One boto pushed its nose up against her outstretched hand.

The clearing was awash in the champagne sounds of pink dolphins and Mata's laughter.

Dennis stretched out his hand.

And one of the dolphins bit him. He yelled and pulled his hand away. Mata grabbed the first aid kit from beneath the seat.

"Is it bleeding?" she asked.

He shook his hand, then stopped and looked at it. "No, but it hurts."

Mata glanced at the river. The dolphins were gone.

"At least you got to see the dolphins," she said.

"I guess I did."

Mata rowed back through the forest. She pointed out macaws, egrets, parrots, white orchids, fig trees. Dennis listened quietly when she talked. Mata moved closer to him, hoping to smell him, or accidentally touch him.

"How did you come to study the botos?" Mata asked.

"I fell in love with them the very first time I saw them," he said. "I guess I've always liked pink. I started studying them in an aquarium actually, and I wanted to see what they were like in the wild."

"There are botos in aquariums?" She shuddered. "That would be like prison."

"Exactly. I'm glad to see them in their natural habitat, but it might be impossible to continue my studies here."

"Why?"

"I study their reproductive cycle. I don't know if I can really observe that entire process here. They're very sensual animals, you know. We documented one couple who had sex nearly forty times in three hours."

"Oh, I've seen them do it more than that," Mata said.

Dennis laughed. She smiled. He leaned toward her, as if to kiss her.

"Hey, you there, can you help me?"

Dennis and Mata turned and looked out into the forest. A very white woman was sitting—naked—on a branch in one of the trees.

"Could you help me?" she asked. "My boat overturned

and the piranhas got everything, including my clothes—
and a piece of my arse, I think. I'm completely helpless."
She smiled.

Mata doubted she was helpless at all.

The blond man's mouth was open. Mata rolled her eyes
and steered the boat to the woman. When they were beneath her, she deftly dropped out of the tree. Dennis took
off his shirt—revealing a pale slightly flabby chest—and
gave it to the woman.

"Thank you, love," she said as she buttoned the shirt
and sat on its tail.

Mata tried to discreetly look for a blow hole, but she
couldn't see the top of the woman's head.

"How'd your boat sink?" Mata asked.

"I stood up," she said. "Silly me. To reach for a fig of
all things."

"Who are you with?" Mata asked.

"I'm visiting friends."

"I know everyone, and I haven't heard of any visitors,"
Mata said.

"Isn't that fine for you," the woman said. "Your grandmother lets you out on the river with strange men?"

"She does. And how do you know—"

"And you, young man," she said. "Your mother lets you
out in the river with a strange young woman?"

He laughed awkwardly. Mata wished he would shut his
mouth: The naked woman was no longer naked, after all.
She sighed.

"I'll take you home," Mata said to the woman. She started the motor. "Maybe Uncle Jaco can find your friends."

"Jaco." The woman sighed his name. "Oh look. There they are. I'll just swim to my friends."

Before Mata could say anything, the woman got up and dived into the water.

"Wait! What?" Dennis said. "Should I jump in after her?"

"No," Mata said. "Look. In the distance. I see other people. She's all right."

"That was strange," Dennis said.

"She was probably an Encantado," Mata said.

"A what?"

"I thought you studied the botos," Mata said.

"Yes, but I don't know what an Encantado is."

"The botos are called the Encantados. They live in a city beneath these waters where everything is like it is here—only so much better. The thing to remember is that they are tricksters and you must not go with them, and don't ever eat anything a boto offers you. Ever. Otherwise you can never come back here and be normal. If you go to the Encante and you're hungry and you eat something a boto offers you, you'll always be hungry. Or if you're sad, you'll always be sad. If you're in love, you'll always be in love."

"That wouldn't be so bad."

"Yes, it would. It wouldn't be a natural love. It would be a terrible ache."

"Sounds like you know your way around. You must know a safe way to the Encante."

She shook her head. "I don't think there is a safe way."

She squinted, trying to find the woman amidst the trees. She couldn't see the white people any more. Perhaps it had all been a mirage—or a hallucination. She looked at Dennis. He smiled. He was so pretty. Even without his shirt. She leaned over and kissed him. Then she sat back and gazed at him.

Kissing him was a bit nicer than kissing other boys. Most of the boys here she had known all her life so kissing them was a bit like kissing a brother—or herself in the mirror.

"That was nice," Dennis said.

Mata reached over and pinched the top of his hand.

"Ouch," he said. "What did you do that for?"

"I was checking to see if I was hallucinating or dreaming," she said.

"I don't think that's how it works. Aren't you supposed to pinch yourself?"

Mata smiled. Then she steered them toward home.

Mata told her grandmother about the naked woman.

Grandmother shook her head. "This is bad. Don't let her near you again."

Uncle Jaco came onto the house.

"She has a boto-woman after her," Grandmother said.

"Mom, you should tell her."

"Tell me what?"

"Tell her what?" Grandmother snapped.

"You're being too hard," Jaco said. "If you just accepted the way things are, maybe you'd feel more at home here."

"I have already lost one son to this," Grandmother said.

"He's not lost!" Mata said. "You said you know where he is. He just ran away. Like a coward. I am not running away."

"You better think about lying down with this Dennis boy and getting away from here," Grandmother said.

"Mom!"

"Grandma, what is wrong with you?"

"You don't know anything about Dennis," Uncle Jaco said. "How can you say such a thing to her?"

Grandmother started to walk away. Then she turned around and shook a finger at Mata.

"If you go with that boto-woman, your life will never be yours again!"

"Is it mine now? When is the last time I made a decision about my own life? I'm an adult, Grandmother."

Mata stamped her foot and turned to look at the river. More than anything she wanted to jump into the water. She knew she couldn't. The Solimões could wound or kill her. She sighed and gazed up at the sky. She suddenly felt trapped. Maybe it was time to leave the river.

"Chaaaa!" she heard.

She looked down. A pink dolphin looked up at her. They stared at one another. Then the boto sank out of sight.

Mata took Dennis out in the boat several more times. They

saw a few dolphins but nothing like that first day. One afternoon when Mata returned to the house, she heard her grandmother arguing with someone. Mata stayed at the edge of the house, dangling her feet near the water, until Ramon Perez, the shaman, came out and climbed down into his boat.

"Hello, Ramon."

"Hello, Mata."

"Is everything all right?" Mata asked.

"Your grandmother wanted me to keep the botos away from you. I told her I could not stop the natural progression of things." Ramon nodded, then started his motor and left her alone.

A shadow fell over the water. Mata looked up.

"It's going to be all right, Grandma," she said.

Her grandmother walked away.

One night Jaco, Grandmother, and Mata got ready to go to a party at Pedro and Sandy's house to celebrate their daughter's one year birthday. Mata put on a pale pink dress. When her grandmother saw her, she said, "What is that color? I don't like it. What about your nice black dress?"

"It's a party, Mom," Jaco said. "Not a funeral. You look fine, Mata."

Jaco rowed them over to Pedro and Sandy's place. Mata heard the music and saw the lights long before they reached the houseboat. Once there, Jaco helped the women out of the boat; then he disappeared into the crowd.

"Where's the baby?" Grandmother asked as she embraced Sandy.

"Safely tucked into her bed away from these maniacs!" she said.

Mata wandered away, looking for Dennis. She walked around the dancers. Most of the men wore hats. Her grandmother would never allow that in her house—too much chance of a boto-man or woman sneaking in. She finally saw Dennis in a corner by the railing with that Diana woman. They were kissing. She watched for a second and was surprised when tears welled up in her eyes.

She turned away.

On the other side of the room, near the steps leading up from the water to the house, the naked woman stood. Only she wasn't naked; she was dressed in a white suit—cream-colored actually—with a jacket, slacks, and big white hat. She smiled at Mata.

Mata started walking toward her. Dennis was obviously not interested in her, and her grandmother was trying to send her away. What harm could it do to talk to this woman?

As she neared the woman, her grandmother stepped between them. Mata saw the woman's lips moving, but she couldn't hear anything above the music. Then suddenly her grandmother reached out and pushed the woman. Startled, the woman tried to get her footing, but Grandmother pushed her again. The woman tipped over backward and fell into the black water.

Someone screamed.

The music stopped.

Several men jumped into their boats and fanned the water with their oars. The partygoers gathered at the railings to watch.

Mata stepped away from the others. Jaco came and stood next to her.

"Why did Grandma do that?" Mata asked. "Who is that woman?"

"That woman is your mother," Jaco said.

"What are you talking about? Momma is dead."

"I'm sorry. They should have told you a long time ago. Your mother didn't die—she was banished from here. Your mother came to a party like this one eighteen plus years ago. She had heard your father was quite the ladies' man so she wanted to teach him a lesson. You know how the Encantados are. Instead she fell in love and got pregnant. Your grandmother and mother agreed it would be best for your grandmother to raise you until you were old enough to decide where you wanted to be. She wouldn't even let your momma breast-feed you."

"Because you never eat food offered by a boto," Mata said.

"That's right."

Dennis walked up to them.

"You look like you've seen a ghost," he said to Mata. "Are you all right?"

"No. The mother I thought was dead may have just drowned!"

"Mata," Uncle Jaco said. "Your grandmother didn't

hurt your mother. The river won't harm her."

"Grandmother should have told me. My mother should have told me." She looked at Dennis. "Will you take me home?"

He shrugged. "Why not?"

The research house was deserted. Everyone was still at the party.

"You want something to drink?" Dennis asked.

Mata sat in one of the empty chairs. She had never been here as a guest before. Her head pounded. She could barely think.

"Mata?"

"No, I don't drink," she said.

He handed her a glass of something, and she gulped it.

He sat next to her. "What happened?"

"I'm a dolphin," she said.

He laughed. "Well, I came here to find dolphins. I guess I got the prettiest one. Pretty in pink."

"I'm not pink," she said. "I told you I don't drink. What is this?"

"I thought it would help calm you," he said.

She drank the rest of whatever had been in the glass. "I don't need to be calm." She felt suddenly dizzy. This was why she did not drink.

"Why is it so dark?" she asked.

"I turned down the lights," Dennis said. "I thought it would be cozier."

"All my life I wanted parents," Mata said. Her tongue

                                                  

felt thick, dry. "Now I find out my mom is alive! Where has she been all these years? Didn't she know I was practically an orphan!"

Dennis leaned over and kissed her.

"Dennis," she said, pushing him away. "I'm trying to talk to you. I don't feel well."

She was moving. Or the world was spinning. Something was wrong.

"Wait. Dennis. Get off me!"

What was happening to her? Why was he grabbing at her clothes?

"Dennis!"

"Ohhhh!" Dennis fell off Mata. She crawled away from him. *What was happening?* Someone turned on the lights.

"Ooowww," Mata said.

"Hey," Dennis said. "You didn't have to kick me there." His voice was too high.

Mata squinted. The white woman who was no longer naked stood over Dennis holding a frying pan while Mata's grandmother moved her foot away from the blond man's prone body.

"I told you to warn her against this boy," the white woman said. "I heard him the first night talking with one of the others, making a bet he could have sex with one of the local girls in a week. Disgusting."

"I didn't get a chance to tell her," Grandmother said. "After I pushed you into the river, she came here. And you're not supposed to be here anyway, you know. You promised to leave her alone until she asked for you."

"She never asked for me because you never told her," the white woman said.

Dennis moaned.

The white woman reached over to the table and picked up a piece of mango.

"Sit up," the woman said to Dennis. "Eat this. It'll make you feel better."

Mata watched as Dennis hesitated; then he took the proffered fruit from the boto-woman and ate it.

Did this mean he would hurt forever?

"I'm a woman now," Mata said, trying not to throw up. "I don't need either one of you running my life."

The white woman reached down and touched Mata's shoulder; her dizziness and nausea disappeared.

"What is your name?" Mata asked.

"You can call me Mom," she said.

"Man, you hurt me," Dennis said.

"Don't worry," Mom said. "It ain't permanent. You were saying, daughter, that you didn't need us. What were you going to do with him?"

"Grandma's been trying to get me to run off with him," Mata said.

"I was wrong," Grandma said. "I did not judge his character correctly."

"You've never been good at judging people," Mom said. "Your son is a no-good womanizer, but I would have made you an excellent daughter-in-law." She looked down at Dennis. "And her name means mother and goddess, by the way, you hopeless god of wine." Dennis moaned. "We have very good hearing," she said to Mata.

Mata was once again speechless.

"You said you're a grown-up woman ready to make her own decisions," Mom said. "Do you want to stay here or come with me?"

"I found out you were my mother two seconds ago," Mata said. "Give me a minute. Can't we get to know each other first? You could come for supper, with Grandma, me, and Uncle Jaco. Like a real family."

"I always liked Jaco," Mom said.

"He just divorced your sister," Grandmother said.

"Your sister! Aunt Maria is your sister?"

Mom shrugged. "It wasn't my choice to hide all this from you."

"You're my mother," Mata said. "You should have come and told me."

"I'm not really the parental type," Mom said. "But, if you want us to get to know one another then we'll get to know one other. Now, what can we do to teach this boy a lesson?"

"He told me he wanted to go to the Encante," Mata said.

Mom smiled. "Well, child, I can take him to the enchanted city. I'll bring him back alive, but he won't be bothering any women no more. Come on, boy."

Mata's grandmother and mother helped Dennis stand. They took him to the railing, then looked back at Mata. She went to them, leaned down, and picked up the blond man's feet. Then the three of them pitched him over into the river. He sank into the black without a word.

"I'll see you soon, sugar," Mom said. She kissed Mata on the cheek. Mata smiled. Now she truly was dolphin-kissed.

Then the woman who was her mother leaped into the river.

Mata and Grandmother stood at the railing looking down at the water. Mata pinched her grandmother's arm.

"Ouch," she said. "What'd you do that for?"

"I wondered if I was dreaming," Mata said.

"That's not the way you do it," Grandmother said. She pinched Mata's hand.

"Ouch."

"That's the way," Grandmother said. "I guess you're not dreaming."

Grandmother put her arm around Mata's waist. "I like that dress, Mata. You look good in pink."

"I hope so."

Chaaaaaah!

♦♦♦

I can't remember when I first heard about the pink dolphins of the Amazon, but I was immediately smitten. When I heard about the Encantados and the world under the water where they lived, I was in love: a fairy world in the Amazon River where the bot-os—the pink dolphins—lived in amazing houses and wore fancy clothes. Sometimes they came into our world and we had to be careful because they liked luring human lovers down below.



KIM ANTIEAU

I did a lot of research on the pink dolphins, the Encantados, and the Amazon River. Some of it I got online or in *National Geographic,* but Sy Montgomery's *Journey of the Pink Dolphins* was very helpful, and I mined her bibliography for more sources. I also loved reading Betty Mindlin's anthology *Barbecued Husbands and other stories from the Amazon,* which gave me the flavor of the folk tales coming from the Amazon. "Seeing Pink" is tame compared with many of the bawdy and raucous stories in *Barbecued Husbands.*

# Briar Rose

She opened her eyes to white and realized she knew nothing.

The nurse was white, too.

"Good morning, sugar," the nurse said. "Do you know who you are?"

She shook her head and wondered where the window was. Maybe if she saw the sunlight, maybe if she saw the world really existed, she would know. Silly thought. The world existed. It was she, she was certain, who was not supposed to be.

"Turn over," the nurse said. Her voice was as pretty as anything she could remember. Though that wasn't much.

She turned over. The nurse threw off the covers and pulled up her hospital gown. "Lookie here, girl," the nurse said. "Maybe that will jar your memory."

She looked down at her own bare ass, twisting her head and arching her back. A small rose bloomed on her white butt, its red petals surrounded by a crown of thorns.

She touched it.

"Maybe my name is Rose," she said.

"All right, Rose, honey," the nurse said, putting the hospital gown and covers back over her bare skin. "We don't know who you are either. You came in with glass all over your arms, cut deep."

Rose held up her bandaged arms.

"You said you'd fallen through a plate glass window." The nurse smiled. "We decided to take your word on that and not put you in the psych ward. All you have to do now is eat that shit they call food, rest, and get better. Just whistle if you need anything."

The nurse in white smiled; for a moment, Rose thought she was dressed in shining armor. Rose shook her head and the nurse was gone. She closed her eyes and reached into her memory. Nothing. Except a man with a needle that looked like those wood burners they used in shop class when she was in high school. "Have you come to be transformed?" the man asked.

"I don't think so," she answered. "I just want a rose tattoo." He hummed some tune, Beethoven's Fifth, while he rat-ta-tat-tatted on her backside.

When he was finished, he smoothed a bandage over the

patch of skin and handed her a card with care instructions, as if she had just bought a sweater. She pulled up her pants and went home. Home? She couldn't really see it, only her reflection in the mirror, somehow, as she pulled off the bandage and looked at the scab forming where he had drawn the rose with his needle and ink.

"There now," she said. "I am whole again. I am myself. My body is mine."

Rose opened her eyes and started to call to Nurse White, to tell her she did know something. Instead, she closed her eyes again and went to sleep.

In the morning, after she ate the shit they called food, Rose got out of bed, found her bloodstained clothes, and got dressed. She was frightened until she thought of the rose blooming on her butt, and then she was no longer afraid. She walked into the hallway, got on the elevator, and went down to the lobby. Outside through the revolving doors, Rose saw a world she had never seen before, bright, noisy. White with color. No, bright with color. She reached into her pockets as she went down the street, away from the hospital. She pulled out forty dollars, crumpled up in her front pockets. That was it.

She hummed Tchaikovsky's *1812 Overture* as she walked. Pigeons shadowed her as she went down the street, toward the tall buildings and bridges arching the river or expressway. The pigeons dogged her steps, looking for handouts. As she walked she remembered nothing except the rose, knew nothing except the feel of her own skin under her hand. She smiled. Ignorance was bliss.

When she got downtown, the pigeons swore at her and flew away to the Burger King parking lot. Rose went onto a street called Burnside and walked until she came to a door which said: TATTOOS, CLEAN SURROUNDINGS, NO ONE UNDER 18 ADMITTED. Rose gently pulled off the gauze from her arms. Scabs traced the places the glass had cut. She dropped the gauze and scabs into a garbage can and then pushed the door open and went inside.

The man with the wood burner looked up when she came in. He smiled. He was the man from her memory.

"Sorry, honey, I can't take it off."

"I don't want it off," she said. "I want another one." She stepped past the swinging door and into his domain of stencils and needles, inks and memories. She looked at the drawings on his walls.

"You going to pick from my flash this time? Last visit you wanted something no one else had." He stood next to her and pointed. "There, how about another flower?"

She shook her head. "I want a child. Here on my arm. Do you have a child? I need to remember."

"No, but I can draw one," he said. He had curly black hair and tattoos everywhere she could see. A dragon belched smoke up his right arm. Jupiter surrounded by stars rotated on his left arm. A butterfly flew beneath that.

She followed him to the tattoo place behind his drawing table. He wanted her to lie down, she wanted to sit. He hummed as he cleaned her arm with alcohol, let the air dry it, and then drew a little girl. Rose watched his fingers and arm move and knew that she could do it, too. Draw.

                                    KIM ANTIEAU

Sketch her life. After a time, when no one else came into the shop, he stopped and asked her if she liked the little girl he had drawn.

She looked down at her arm. "That little girl is me," she said.

"Yes," he said, "I know."

"I don't remember if I liked her." The girl was smaller than Rose had imagined, two years old perhaps. The man began spreading the inks onto her arm. Then he sewed the girl into her skin with the color. When he finished, it was dark outside and the little girl was blowing out two candles on a blue-frosted cake.

"Someday, Charlie, my brother, some little prick's going to get her," her uncle Bobbie said, "and it'll all be over. That's the way with girls. Dad always said so." He laughed and spilled beer on himself while her mother sliced pieces of cake. Rose looked over at her father and saw the fear in his eyes; she was only two but she saw it, and Bobbie was too young to drink beer, maybe thirteen.

"Are you all right?" The tattooist touched her arm with his fingers. She moved her arm away from him. "Sorry," he said. "You only want to be touched if it hurts."

She looked at the little girl on her arm. Her lips were pursed, forever trying to blow out the candles.

"Can you teach me how to do this?" she asked.

"Transform yourself? Or tattoo?"

"Draw with a needle."

"Do you have any money?"

"Forty dollars and two memories," she said. "I could

stay here. Clean up. Do anything else you want."

"Don't scratch your tattoo," he said. He started to hand her the card with care instructions written on it. She stared at him.

"All right," he said. He nodded as if he had known it all along.

"I want another," she said. "The other arm. A snake."

He got up and went to the door and locked it. He pulled the shade down. Then he took a stencil from his flash and returned to her. "Turn around," he said, "so I can work on your other side." He pressed the drawing onto her arm. When he pulled it away, Rose could see the outline of a snake. She stared at the bandage on her other arm and imagined the girl beneath it while the tattooist drew the snake.

When he was finished, he dropped his instruments. "I can't do any more," he said and walked up the steps that led to his loft. She listened to his heavy breathing for several minutes before she got up. She threw out the needle and put away the inks. Then she went into a small office in the back and curled up on a battered couch.

When she awakened, it was still dark. She felt hurried, as if something had to be finished soon. Something she had started and somehow had messed up. She turned on a light over the desk and looked at her arms. Where the glass had pierced her skin were now black lines, jagged shapes tattooed into her arms.

She remembered standing in the motel room, wondering why she was there. Her mother was dead. Too many sleeping pills. Her father was dead. Too many cigarettes. And she was alive. Her body ached. Her body that wasn't hers. The tattoo itched. It had not brought her back from the edge. Something had pricked her, just as her father had feared: men, boys, life. She hurt, as if slivers of glass were tickling her insides. She had raised her fists in anger, wanted to pound on the windows that looked out onto the parking lot, when suddenly she knew how to have peace.

She ended up in the hospital eating shit and getting sponge baths from Nurse White.

She turned her arms around and pulled off the bandage over the little girl and her birthday cake. The scab came off with the bandage. The girl had tears in her eyes. She had heard the conversation, had known her life had changed.

Rose peeled off the other bandage. The snake shed his scab, and Rose was in the backyard of her home, eight years old, bent over a translucent snake skin, wondering where the snake had gone. What an easy life. If you don't like it, just shed it and begin anew. She reached out a finger and touched the skin tentatively. Dry.

"If it's from a poisonous snake you could die." She looked up. Uncle Bobbie. He smiled. All his smiles looked monstrous. She wasn't sure why. He snatched up the snake skin and began running. She went after him, into the woods where the oaks and maples were shedding their leaves. Suddenly his footsteps stopped and she was alone in the woods. Then Bobbie jumped from behind a tree and threw her to the ground, laughing all the time, tossing the snake skin into the air, out of her reach. He pulled off her pants and then his. When it was over, he promised to get her a pony if she didn't tell anyone.

Rose turned off the light. Now she had four memories.

She watched the man prick pictures into other people's skins all day. She took care of his inks and needles and cleaned the floors. At night, she counted his money and gave it to him. He needled her when everyone was gone. A drop of blood tattooed on her right forearm brought Bobbie back to her, brought his smile as he zipped up his pants and she put her hands between her legs. She cried and he told her to shut up. Her parents were afraid to leave her with anyone else except family. Afraid of the outside world. Uncle Bobbie had been right, they would tell each other, there were millions of guys out there just waiting to hurt their child.

A willow tree brought her father back. She leaned her head against his knee. He stroked her hair while he read his newspaper. Her mother knelt in her garden and whispered to the flowers.

"I've never seen anyone heal as quickly as you do," the tattooist told her. He seemed tired, as if he felt it all, too.

She nodded and took the needle from him. "May I try?"

"Don't hurt yourself," he said.

"Isn't that what this is all about?" she asked, holding the needle like a writer holds a pen, poised to express herself.

"No," he said. And he went up the steps. She waited until she heard his heavy breathing, and then she began drawing.

  

She tried a flower, but it turned into a warped sun, bringing back a summer when she was four and Bobbie was pushing his fingers between her legs while he held onto something between his legs. Rose laughed at his face, funny Bobbie, until he hurt her and she started to cry and wondered where her mother was. The sun was too hot and the flowers were dying.

"Momma," she whispered.

She tried tattooing flowers again, this time on her thighs. First violets, then roses, gardenias, rhodies; a garden bloomed on her skin and she was next to her mother in the dirt. Her mother was crying, the tears making paths through the dust on her face. "What's wrong? What's wrong?" Rose asked. She was ten and her throat hurt from trying not to cry. Bobbie lurked in the bushes somewhere, always waiting, and Momma cried.

The tattooist came down the stairs when it was morning. He looked at her thighs.

"You're an artist," he said.

"The agony and the ecstasy?" she said. "I'm my own Sistine Chapel." She held up the needle. "Will you do my back?"

"Why?"

"I have to remember," she said.

"But wasn't it nice before?" he said. "When you knew nothing?"

She shook her head. "I knew nothing when I was two years old and look what happened."

"You hardly scab," he said.

"I go straight to scarring," she said.

She took off her shirt and camisole. She didn't care if he saw her. He poked holes in her back and let the ink soak in, making the memories permanent. They could be wiped from her brain but not from her skin.

"What have you drawn?" she asked when he paused.

"Can't you tell?" he said. "Don't you remember being a kid in the bathtub with your brother or sister? You'd wipe the other guy's back and then put soap on it and draw, usually words, and the other person would have to guess."

"I didn't have any brothers and sisters," she said. "But I do remember a cousin, Mary, and we played together. Sometimes we took baths together when we were real little and we'd do that. Yes, I remember now." It had been nice to touch her and to be touched by her. They were each the other's drawing boards. They got water and soap everywhere. "We floated little plastic ships in the water and pretended we were seeing the world."

"That's what I put on your back," he said.

She got up and went into the bathroom where there was a full-length mirror and looked at herself. Two girls stood on a sailing ship. They held hands and waved to the mermaids in the water. The ship bobbed in the waves. A flag with a rose on it flapped in the breeze.

Rose smiled. Some of the memories were good.

She went back into the room where the tattooist sat.

"You understand that I have to do this," she said.

"Yes," he said. "It's part of what I do. Transformations, remember. It's difficult sometimes."

   

She nodded.

She drew a lady on her left calf. Her golden hair flowed away from her as she lay on the bed of skin. Her eyes were open but Rose knew she was dead. Her open eyes had surprised Rose. She had died of an overdose of pills. Eaten one at a time.

"Why?" Rose asked as her mother swallowed a little white pill.

"Because I ache," she said. "I've been stabbed in a million places."

Had Bobbie played with her, too?

"I need you to stay," Rose said. She started to cry. Where was her father? At work? The car was with him. Their closest neighbors, the Nelsons, were gone on vacation. She wasn't sure she could reach anyone else. They lived too far from the city. Out in the country where nothing could hurt them. Her mother had ripped out the phone.

"Bobbie's been playing with me," Rose said. She was twelve, desperate. She'd tell her mother, get her to stay.

"What do you mean?" Her mother swallowed four pills this time.

"You know, putting his thing in me," Rose said. Stop it, Mom. Stay with me.

"Tell your father," she said. "He'll protect you."

That was it. That was all her mother had to say to her after all the agony she had been through.

"He promised me a pony," she said.

"I'm so tired," her mother said.

Rose ran downstairs and out the door. She ran into the

dusty afternoon and through the woods toward the house Bobbie shared with his parents, farther and farther away from home. He worked in town at night. Maybe he'd be home now. She pounded and pounded on the door. After a while, she heard his voice from deep within the house. He came to the door, half asleep.

"What are you doing here?" he said.

"It's Momma," she said. "She's taking too many sleeping pills. Please, you've got to do something."

He opened the screen door and she came in. He went to the phone and called the police and an ambulance. She hated him, despised him, hated herself. But he was going to save her mother.

He took her hand, and they went out to his car. He drove her back to her house and together they went upstairs. Her mother lay on the bed, her hair spread out around her, like a golden-haired Snow White waiting for her Prince Charming. Her eyes were open.

Bobbie started to cry. Rose went away. She wasn't certain where she went. Her soul wandered for a time. She thought she had died when she was eight, but she had been wrong. Now she died. Pricked by her mother's death.

She drew a garden on her other leg. Its weeds and thorns twisted around her calf and up her knee. A man stood among the weeds.

"He never let me near him after that," Rose said.

"Who? Your father?" the tattooist asked.

"No," Rose said. Tears stung her eyes. "Bobbie."

She felt like she was going to throw up. "I hated him,

                                   

but he was all there was. I guess. Momma had left me a long time before she died. And my dad was . . . my dad."

The tattooist took the needle. Rose lay on her stomach, and he drew on her back. Her butt became a tangle of dark briar that went up her back, no way to get through.

She remembered leaving her bedroom window open. The boys knew where to come in and they did, one at a time. She didn't care who they were. She just opened her legs to them. She had to fill the emptiness somehow.

The briars pricked her skin; the tattooist drew drops of blood down her legs.

She touched the blood and remembered being seventeen. Her father was drunk. She had never seen him drunk before. But he was blind with grief. He wept and started calling her Joanie. Her mother's name. She went into the bathroom and curled her hair up and behind her, dabbed her cheeks with powder, put her mother's pearl necklace around her neck, slipped into her mother's blue flowered dress, the one her mother had worn often, especially when she was in the garden, and then she went out to her father. In the darkness, she opened herself to him, not understanding, and he pushed into her, sobbing, until in the middle of it, hard inside her, he opened his eyes and screamed with the horror of it, knowing it was Rose; knowing it, he kept going. When he was finished, he curled up on the floor and asked how she could have done it.

"Does it hurt?" the tattooist asked.

"Yes." Rose wiped her tears and sat up. "I want you to do my breasts."

He drew flowers and restaurants and neon lights and cowboys. It hurt. He drew her trek across the country after her father told her to leave. She went to Bobbie's house first. He had a wife and a child and he could not look at her. Rose turned away from the house and hoped he never touched his little girl the way he had touched her. She took a ride from a trucker. She let him have her at night, after they drove several hundred miles. She felt dry inside, and he told her she wasn't much fun. "I don't want nobody don't want me," he said. He let her out in the darkness. The next one beat her up. The tattooist pricked the black and blue spot on her skin. She hadn't minded the beatings so much. She deserved it. Touching was meant to hurt. She ended up working in a restaurant in Tucson, fifteen hundred miles from home. For some reason, she told Bobbie where she was.

She looked down at her breasts and saw the envelope, saw the writing on the letter. The tattooist bit his lip as he pushed the needle into her.

"It's for my own good," she said.

"It's for your death," he said.

She nodded.

The letter told her her father was dead. A year to the day she had left. Lung cancer. She didn't go back for the funeral. She stayed in Tucson. A cactus grew from her navel. An old Indian woman tried to heal her insides. But she couldn't let the woman touch her. Couldn't let anyone touch her.

When she turned nineteen, she went north. She found

the tattooist and had him etch a rose into her body. It was her body now.

He painted the house around her side. It wrapped her. She had never gone back to the house. She had heard they sold it. Another family lived in it now. After she got the rose, she thought it would be better. It was supposed to be better. A reason to go on: because she had reclaimed her body. Instead, she stood in the motel room and wanted to die.

The tattooist moved away from her. He was crying.

"There are scabs all over your body," he said.

She was naked except for the tattoos.

"Are you glad you remembered?" he asked.

"No," she said. "Thank you."

"Don't go," he said. "You're very good. An artist. You could transform people."

"I can't even transform myself," she said. She put on her clothes. Her entire body hurt.

"I could help you get started," he said. She was quiet. "Stay until the scabs are gone then."

"All right," she said. "I'll at least stay the night."

He started to touch her arm, but he stopped. "I'm going to bed," he said. He slowly walked up the steps to his loft.

Rose went to the office and sat on the couch. Her body was now covered with her memories. It ached with them. She took off her shirt; the throbbing lessened somewhat. She wanted to cry. The memories burned her skin. Hurt. Too much. She stood up and took off her pants. How could she live with it all? Stand it? She touched one of the faces on her body that was Bobbie. He peered at her from her right shoulder. She shook herself, like a dog shaking water from its fur, and the scabs fell away from her body, becoming flower petals, red, yellow, blue, floating slowly to rest on the carpet. Now she could clearly see all her memories. Her life was etched into her skin. She went into the bathroom and stared at her body in the mirror. Her ruined body. Bobbie had ruined her. Killed her. Doomed her to sleep until she died. Her mother had ruined her. Her father had ruined her. She had only been a child. They had all taken pieces of her and had forgotten to give them back.

She started to cry. She thought of those hours when she hadn't remembered anything. When Nurse White had turned her over. A babe from the womb. Being cared for, loved, patted. She had known nothing. Now she knew everything.

Bobbie drank too much. His wife had left him. Her father was dead, never forgiving her. Never realizing it had been his responsibility, not his daughter's. Her mother was dead. Never caring what she left behind.

"Time to wake up," Rose whispered to her reflection.

She reached down and pulled a briar away from the patch that circled the rose on her butt. Her skin itched. Crackled. She sat on the floor and pressed the thorn into the top of her head until she drew blood. It had been good to remember. Blood ran into her eyes. To realize she had only been a child. Her mother had chosen to die; Bobbie had chosen to hurt her; her father had chosen to blame her.

                                                    

It was past. Time for reclamation. Seeing it all had made it, somehow, understandable. She remembered touching the snake skin when she was a child, being amazed that it could just start fresh, shed its old life.

She stretched and creaked and rubbed herself along the carpet, and her past started to fall from her. She sat up and helped it: she peeled away the dead skin. It felt dry and cool, just as the snake skin had. Lifeless. No power. The flowers came away, Bobbie's face, her mother's eyes, the weeds, the ship on her back, the snake, the blood. All of it. She stood and dropped the past onto the carpet. She shook herself, causing the last pieces of scabs to fly away. She looked down at her body. She was white and pink. New. Only the rose on her buttock remained, without the crown of thorns.

The tattooist stood in the doorway. He leaned over and picked up the skin.

Rose touched his arm. "Leave it," she said. "I don't need it anymore." She reached down and smoothed her hand over her rose tattoo and smiled. "I am myself again."

♦♦♦

This story is one of my favorites, and one of my readers' favorites, judging from the letters I get about it. I wrote it after a long bout with illness when I thought I would never write short stories again. I made it into a little chapbook and sent it out to family and friends before it got published. I sent it out to a lot of places, I think, before Dennis Etchison picked it up for his amazing *Metahorror* anthology. Unfortunately, the art in the antho was so disturbing that I've never been able to look at the book all the way through. To this day, I can't look at it, although I was proud to be in it and to be in the company of some amazing authors. "Briar Rose" was reprinted in the *Year's Best Horror Stories: 21*. We later reprinted it in *Daughters of Nyx* and on *Furious Spinner. The Journal of Mythic Arts* reprinted it in 2005.

I have been fascinated with the story of Sleeping Beauty/ Briar Rose since I was a child. It seemed so awful to have a chance accident cause you to fall asleep and miss your whole life. Especially given that it could have all been prevented if your guardians had been better caretakers. I've often wanted to expand this story into a novel. But it's an intense place to be, and I'm not sure I could be in that place for an entire novel.

But I do love this story.

# Dragon Pearl

Once upon a time, a shy young woman named Pearl lived with and cared for her parents and their farm for many years. Then they both became ill and acted unkindly toward their daughter. They ordered her around and complained about every meal she prepared for them. They said she was too loud and clumsy, even when she was as quiet and careful as a mouse.

Several days before the longest night of the year, Pearl visited the healer who lived at the edge of the forest. She asked the healer to help her parents get well. The healer told Pearl she could easily make a potion to heal Pearl's parents, but she was out of one crucial ingredient.

"I—I will get it, whatever it is." Pearl stammered because she was not accustomed to talking with strangers.

"Bring me back the dragon pearl from the dragon on the Eastern Mountain Where the Red Poppies Grow."

Pearl gasped. Everyone knew that a dragon pearl was priceless and could cure any ill, and a dragon would die—and kill—to protect it. It was said every dragon carried the dragon pearl in a tiny pouch in her throat.

"I will go," said Pearl, even though she had never even been out of her village.

"Once you are in the forest," the healer advised, "you must pick up the first thing you see that does not appear to belong. Take it with you. That is your talisman and it will bring you great luck during your journey."

Pearl left the healer and went into the forest. She was afraid of all the strange noises she heard, but she travelled on. Soon enough she saw something on the ground that did not look like it belonged. She bent over and picked up a small round blue ordinary-looking button. She rubbed it to see if a genie would come out; she whispered to it to see if her wishes might come true, but nothing out of the ordinary happened. Nevertheless, she tucked the button into a safe place in her knapsack and kept walking.

Since this is the short version of Pearl's story, I will say at this point that she had many great adventures which tried her strength, patience, and ingenuity. But she continued on her way to the Eastern Mountain Where the Red Poppies Grow.

One day she had to walk many hours in a terrible snowstorm. She came to a woman huddled on the side of the road. Pearl asked if she needed help. The woman said, "I am so cold. My coat will not stay closed." Pearl looked and could see the woman was freezing because she had lost a button on her coat. While the woman ate the food and drank the water Pearl offered her, Pearl reached into her knapsack and pulled out her sewing kit. She had no extra buttons, so she retrieved the magical blue button she had found on the forest floor and sewed it onto the woman's coat.

"Ahhh, that is much better," the woman said. "I thank you."

She went on her way, and Pearl went on hers.

The next day, the snow melted and Pearl came to the village at the bottom of the Eastern Mountain Where the Red Poppies Grow. She asked the first person she saw where the dragon lived, but he would not tell her. No one would. As everyone knows, any town worth its salt has a dragon to protect its assets and give the occasional speech and light the bonfire during ceremonies—and the villagers don't want strangers bothering their dragon or trying to lure it away with promises of shinier pastures, so to speak. Pearl went to the castle where the queen lived. Perhaps the queen would be more understanding about her plight and tell her where the dragon was.

"It is you," the queen said when she opened the door to Pearl's insistent knocking.

"It is you," Pearl said, nodding to the woman whose coat she had fixed only the day before.

"I owe you my life," the queen said after Pearl told her why she wanted to see the dragon, "so I will do you this favor and tell you where the dragon is, although I warn you, we haven't seen much of the dragon lately."

As soon as the queen told Pearl the way, Pearl ran right up the Eastern Mountain Where the Red Poppies Grow and found the dragon pacing alongside a clear placid lake. The dragon was ruby red in color and roared fire when it saw Pearl.

"Please, Mr. Dragon, don't hurt me," Pearl said, holding up her hands. "It is urgent that you help me."

"Hah! It is always urgent," the dragon roared. "And I—I am not *Mister* Dragon, thank you. *That* was my uncle and he died and I was the only one even halfway qualified to take this job! I—I didn't want it!"

The dragon stammered just like Pearl used to when she was nervous.

"What can I call you then?" Pearl asked.

"Ruby Red," the dragon said. "Now what do you want?"

"My parents are ill and the healer said she can heal them if she has your dragon pearl for her potion."

The dragon's eyes narrowed and Pearl thought she was just about to burn her alive.

Instead, Ruby Red replied, "I see you are in great need. I will help you if you will help me. You seem like an articulate person. I am supposed to give a speech at tomorrow's Solstice celebration. I *loathe* giving speeches. I don't like crowds either. All that touching and talking. If I could just come in, light the bonfire, and leave. Actually, I don't want to do that either, but what's a dragon to do?"

Pearl agreed she would give the speech; in return, the dragon would give her the dragon pearl.

Pearl went down the mountain and practiced her speech all night. Midday, the villagers began to gather at the town center. They told stories, sang, and ate until the sun went down. When it was dark, Pearl went and stood by the unlit bonfire with the villagers. Suddenly, she heard the whush, whush, whush of the dragon's wings and looked up. It was so dark she could see nothing except the dragon's slit orange eyes that looked like two crescent moons. With a thud Ruby Red landed behind Pearl and opened her mouth just enough so that Pearl was backlit by her throaty fire.

"Your dragon, Miss Ruby Red, has a touch of laryngitis," Pearl said. "So I will speak on her behalf tonight. She wanted me to tell you that she is proud and pleased to follow in her uncle's footsteps and protect the assets of your fine town. She will do whatever she can to fulfill her duties. She wishes you all good health and prosperity for the new year."

With that, Ruby Red opened her jaws wide and spit fire onto the waiting bonfire sticks until they caught fire. The crowd roared with pleasure as the flames leapt into the darkness. Then the dragon jumped into the air and flew away.

The villagers ate, told stories, and drummed until the darkness turned gray. Until the sun became an orange-red sliver on the horizon like a dragon's eye. The villagers cheered the rising sun, then went home to bed.

Pearl climbed the mountain again.

"I have come for the dragon pearl," Pearl told Ruby Red.

The dragon hung her head. "I have to confess something to you."

Butterflies fluttered in Pearl's stomach.

"There is no dragon pearl," the dragon said. "It's a myth. I'm so sorry I deceived you."

Pearl gasped. "No! That can't be true. Everyone knows about the dragon pearl."

Ruby Red nodded. "Yes, everyone knows about the Philosopher's Stone, too, but no one has ever seen it. If a dragon pearl exists I have never seen one. You can have any of my treasures. There are lots of pearls. Technically, you could call any of those pearls dragon pearls since I—a dragon—guard them."

Pearl was inconsolable. Now her parents would never be healed.

"You can stay here with me," the dragon offered. "We could protect the villagers together. A team. You the words. Me the fire. Tell me what I can do to help you."

"Take me back to the healer's cottage."

The dragon nodded. Pearl climbed into the pouch in the dragon's huge throat—there really was a pouch, just no pearl—and minutes later she was standing alone in the forest near the healer's cottage. She listened to the sounds of the woods and realized she was no longer afraid of what she heard or saw.

She went into the healer's cottage and told the woman her story.

"I have failed," Pearl said.

The healer shook her head. "I asked you to bring me the dragon pearl and so you have. I finally see before me the person I midwifed into this world, the person I named Dragon Pearl. You have found she who is you. You are now no longer in need of the healing potion."

"Dragon Pearl?"

"That was your given name."

"My parents never told me," Pearl said.

"Your parents have always underestimated you," the healer said. "They do not understand your true nature."

Pearl wasn't certain she understood her true nature either, yet she did feel greatly changed by her journey. She thanked the healer and returned home. As she walked up the path to her house, she could see that the farm had been well tended in her absence. The animals looked healthy. Someone had patched the barn roof.

She went inside the house. Her mother stirred a pot of soup hanging over the fire. Her father stood at the table cutting up vegetables. They looked healthy and vigorous as they talked, laughed, and worked. They turned around when Pearl said hello.

"Oh, it is so good you are home," her mother said. "We have had to do so much on our own."

"Yes, there's so much to do, little Pearl," her father said. "Why did you desert us?"

Pearl smiled as her parents sat at the table and looked

disapprovingly at her.

"I have come only for a visit," Pearl said. "It is good to see you well again."

"No thanks to you," her father said.

"Yes, no thanks to me," Pearl said.

Pearl ate dinner with her parents and told them of her travels. In the morning she packed her knapsack and kissed her parents.

"Good-bye, Dragon Pearl," her parents called as she left.

Dragon Pearl waved good-bye. She returned to the Eastern Mountain Where the Red Poppies Grow. She became known for her eloquent speeches and fascinating stories. People came from all around to participate in the ceremonies she and Ruby Red Dragon officiated. She had many adventures, near and far, and lived happily ever after.

♦♦♦

This story was inspired by Clarissa Pinkola Estes's retelling of the "Crescent Moon Bear." In it, a wife has to go through a perilous journey to get a hair from the Crescent Moon Bear so the village healer can make a potion to cure the woman's husband who has been sick and miserable since he came home from the war. I had also read about the mythical dragon pearl which Asian dragons had either on their foreheads or under their chins. It was supposed to be quite valuable and healing if one could procure it. Instead of searching for the hair of a bear, my hera had to go looking for a dragon pearl.

We made this into a chapbook one Solstice and gave it to family and friends. I sewed a button into the last page of each chapbook. At our Solstice party, I read it out loud to the group. It was great fun.

# Rose Red and Snow White

Skin as white as Virgin snow.
Ice crystals grown from dust motes,
Specks of Earth thrown skyward:
*Snow White*
Lips as red as pricked blood, first blood,
Unfolding like the Virgin Rose,
Whole in and of herself:
*Rose Red*
Colors of the Goddess,
Clues this tale is more than it seems.
*Aren't they all?*
When Le Bête knocks on their door

Mid-winter, matted ice and snow giving him
A Rasti look, the twin goddesses invite
The Wild in,
Serve him tea and comb his fur.
*No sign of gold at first blush.*
Then what? Did they watch Jack Frost
Breathe on their windows and listen to
Ice crack into wintry art?
*Their version of cable.*
Today, would they gulp beer, eat chips,
And watch television, the three of them?
Would Le Bête complain about the
Commercialization of all things sacred
As he clutched the remote?
"Let's live off the grid," he'd murmur
While Snow White and Rose Red painted
Their fingernails black as pitch and their lips
Red as a whore's candied tongue.
*Goth or harlot?*
Or, perhaps before the Bear enters their domain
The sisters are hippie-girls, wandering, modern-like,
Looking for some *thing*. Hitching rides.
Living off the land. Eating huckleberries plucked
From their core, the juice staining their lips and teeth
Deep purple. Watching the bloody salmon leap,
They wonder why their mouths water, wonder
What it is they have lost.
*Why does it ache so much?*
So when a man in gold knocks on their door



KIM ANTIEAU

Mid-winter, they pull him inside, shining him on.

Until they spot the fur beneath the gold.

*Le Bête!*

They speak in tongues as they

Rip the clothes from him.

*He is only a symbol, after all.*

The sisters bury their faces in his fur.

When they look down at their own bodies,

They see they have grown Grizzly claws.

They laugh and embrace each other.

The man, speechless, tries to piece his

Gold suit back together. Alone

In the empty cottage, he closes the door.

*Outside, the night is wild with beasts.*

♦♦♦

When I was a child, the Grimm's fairy tale "Red Rose and Snow White" was my favorite fairy tale. I'm not certain why: except whenever the bear ripped his fur and we could see gold beneath, it made me shiver with delight and expectation.

I wrote this poem on the road. Mario and I were driving to the coast of Oregon from the Columbia River Gorge, and I had this idea and had to write it. I normally get quite car sick if I read or write in the car, but I was able to do it. I sent it to the *Journal of Mythic Arts* soon after, and they published it.

# The Señorita
# and the Cactus Thorn

Once upon a dusty time a young woman walked down a long dirt driveway toward the Earth-colored house with a long wide front porch. Beside the house was a paloverde tree, all green to gather in and process the sun, and a mesquite tree, whose roots reached clear down to springs that gurgled up and became rivers in China, or so some supposed; on the other side of the house, a saguaro stood, two arms up as if a bandit was asking for all its cash and bonds. Behind the house in a tall palm tree, an owl asked the young woman, "Who, who?" She held a white umbrella over her head with one hand and carried a small suitcase in her other hand. She wore a long white dress that kept wiping the dirt off her buttoned leather shoes as she walked.

The Woman Who Lived in the House stepped outside, wiping her hands on her apron, and thought, "This woman—this girl—from the city will never last in the desert long enough to marry my *mijo*. No, no."

Everyone who lived anywhere near knew that the Woman Who Lived in the House was a force to be reckoned with. She had lived here for as long as anyone could remember and maybe before. All kinds of stories had circulated about her previous life, before she became the Woman Who Lived in the House. Some said she had been La Llorona, wandering the wash in front of the house wailing, until she spotted the Señor on the porch. He looked cool under the verandah, comfortable, drinking his watermelon juice. He asked her to join him, so she did.

Another tale goes around that she was once Coyote. Before she ran the nearby hills, most coyotes were loners, but she knew where to get the food for the least amount of trouble, and oh, the songs she sang. All the coyotes wanted to be part of her chorus. When she was Coyote, she had known all the magic of the desert and how to trick anyone or anything out of whatever they held precious. One woman said she even tricked her grandmama out of her gold teeth, then gave them back when she couldn't figure out what to do with them. Then she met Señor. Once again he sat on that porch, drinking his juice. And she was smitten. Being that time of month and everything—the full moon—she decided to come and sit for a spell. She had been here ever since.

Whatever story anyone told, everyone believed the Woman Who Lived in the House had once been full of magic. Maybe still was. They didn't take any chances. No one crossed her. All of them would have advised the young woman to go home, no doubt. No man, no matter how beautiful or well-groomed, was worth it.

When the young woman reached the porch, she said, "Señora, I am—"

"I know who you are," the Woman said. "You are the woman who wishes to marry my *mijo*."

"And he wishes to marry me," the Señorita said.

The Woman nodded. "Well, we have three nights to see how suited you are to be his wife and live in this desert."

The Señorita hesitated, still standing on the dusty ground.

"Come," the Woman said, almost as an afterthought, "you are most welcome to my house."

The Señorita smiled and stepped up onto the porch. "I am glad to be here," she said. "I'm looking forward to learning more about your son's life out here. I can't wait to see him."

"He has gone away with his father," the Woman said, "to buy horses on the other side of the mountain. They will not return until three nights have passed. I have much to teach you. You must know how to wash my son's clothes, cook his favorite foods, and survive in the desert. Only then can you be a good wife to my son."

The Woman took the suitcase from the girl, and they

stepped out of the bright sun into the cool house. Outside smelled faintly of mesquite, inside of allspice.

"Your son knows how to wash his own clothes and cook his own favorite meals," the Señorita said. "You have taught him well. He will be a good husband. Still, I am eager to learn all that you can teach me."

"I am not concerned about whether he will be a good husband or not," the Woman said as she led the younger woman down a long hallway to a bedroom. A large window took up most of the east wall, giving the Señorita an excellent view of the desert. The Woman put the suitcase on the bed. "First, you cannot wear those clothes. Look, your dress is already gray at the hem."

"I will change," the Señorita said.

"Yes," the Woman said. "Then we will cook."

After the Señorita put on a darker and shorter dress, she wandered through the long house until she came to the kitchen where her future mother-in-law waited. The woman handed her an apron, which the younger woman put on.

"You are too skinny," the Woman said. "You have to have meat on your bones. You should be bigger, fatter, stronger. More meat keeps the bruises away when you run into things or they run into you."

"I can eat," the Señorita said. "I will gain weight. And I am strong."

"I have already asked for the blessings of the directions," the Woman said, "so we may begin. We'll make *masa* first, then tortillas. Later mole."

"*Masa* for tortillas?" the Señorita asked. She smiled. She had made tortillas many times with her mother. Perhaps her first test would not be so difficult.

"Over there is the ash," the Woman said.

"Ash?"

The Woman looked at her. "You haven't made tortillas before?"

"We always use *masa harina*," she said.

The Woman shook her head. "No, we must have the blessings of the desert, the trees. Their spirit—their ash— is what brings the tortillas into being."

The Señorita resisted the impulse to shrug. She looked into three bowls: one contained water, the other corn, so the third must be ash.

"Mix the ash with the water," the Woman said.

While the ash and corn boiled, they began chopping chiles for the mole: poblanos, serranos, pasillas. Twice the Señorita forgot she was chopping chiles and rubbed her eyes. She tried not to cry out—or cry, but the pain was awful. She felt so stupid. She chopped chiles all the time in the apartment she shared with her mother and grandmother in the city. Well, at least, she watched while they chopped.

The Woman and the Señorita stood in the kitchen for many hours. The Woman asked about the Señorita's family. She said her mother and grandmother thought it was good she was coming out to the desert. They had been desert people once, too, but had had to move away.

"My grandmother says the desert is full of magic," the

Señorita said.

"Hmph, the desert is full of danger," the Woman said as they prepared the masa. "No, no, that's too much water. It can't be too sticky or too dry."

The Señorita was tired at the end of the day. She tried to enjoy the tortillas and mole they had made as they ate a silent dinner together. They had also prepared beans and refried beans, flour tortillas, bread, flan, and a couple of other desserts for another time. She was glad to go to bed.

The Woman Who Lived in the House had to admit—to herself—that the woman from the city had followed her directions very well. She was too skinny and sometimes thoughtless, but she could be a good cook if she tried. She still did not think she was the woman for her son. The Woman started to get into her bed, when suddenly she heard a shriek. And then another. She stepped out of her room to see the Señorita running down the hallway toward her.

"Señora! This house is haunted," she said. "I have heard a ghost. And there are monsters snorting around under the window."

The Woman calmly followed the girl back to her room. She stepped to the window.

"There! Do you hear it?" the Señorita said.

"That is no ghost, you foolish girl," the Woman said. "That is an owl! You've never heard an owl before?"

"And what is that horrible snuffling noise?" the Señorita asked.

"Look, can't you see? They are javelinas! What kind of wife are you to be if a bird and a pig terrify you? They are nothing! We have rattlesnakes and scorpions and heat that'll scorch your skin off. Now those are things to scream about. Good night!"

The Woman went back to her room, leaving the Señorita in the dark. The young woman shut her window and climbed into bed once again. She felt like crying, but she didn't. Tomorrow she would do better.

The next day, the Woman awakened the Señorita early. They went into the desert and gathered prickly pear pads, mesquite pods, cinchweed, and some verbena. Although the Señorita did not know what any of these plants were, she learned quickly and gathered up her fair share. She also seemed to get pricked by a cholla or prickly pear every other step she took. She even got pricked by a saguaro.

At the end of their trek, she felt bruised and battered. She stood on the porch for a long time while the Woman plucked the thorns from her shoes, shirt, and jeans. She put them all in a bowl that was nearly overflowing by the time they were finished.

"What kind of desert wife can you be if you become a porcupine every time you step off this porch?" the Woman said, setting the bowl of cactus thorns on the kitchen counter. "You are too fragile for this place."

"I am not fragile," the Señorita said. "I just need to learn to be more observant."

"Hmph," the Woman Who Lived in the House said.

"Let's observe some horse manure then. The barn needs cleaning."

This was not something the Woman ever did, but she was more and more convinced that this girl from the city was not suitable for the desert, so she showed her how to muck out the stalls and waited for her to refuse such dirty work. The young woman did not refuse. The Woman returned to the house and prepared dinner alone.

That night as the Woman was getting into her bed, the Señorita once again cried out. The Woman went to the room and asked her what was wrong.

"Wild dogs are trying to get into my room," she said. "Listen. They're right at hand."

"Those are not wild dogs," the Woman said. "Those are coyotes. Have you never heard a coyote? They are far away. None would want to come into this room. It is stifling hot." She flung open the window. "How do you suppose you can live in the desert if a coyote howl terrifies you?"

The Señorita said nothing. The sounds of the owl, javelinas, and coyotes seemed to fill the room. How would she ever sleep? She had barely slept the night before. Even though the Woman had told her the noises she heard were only javelinas and an owl, the sounds still kept her awake. Now tonight the coyotes were calling out!

"I am sorry to have troubled you, Señora," she said. "I will go to sleep now."

The Señorita did not sleep well. She even cried a little,

putting her pillow over her face so that she could not be heard. She loved the Woman's son very much, but she did not even know if they would live in the desert. Why was she putting herself through all of this? So far, she did not like the desert, and she wanted to go home. She sighed. Still. She did not want to fail. Maybe the desert wasn't so bad. She did like the birds. She noticed Gila woodpeckers in the saguaros, calling out for all the world to hear. The thrashers were noisy, too, watching them with yellow eyes. And quail ran in front of them, seeming to chastise the women for disturbing them. She liked all the bird chatter; it was more conversation than she got from the Woman.

She got out of bed and helped cook breakfast with the Woman. Then she cleaned the kitchen. Laundry was next. She did not wince as she and the Woman lifted the tubs of water onto the stove, even though her arms and legs shook. After lunch, they went into the garden and gathered squash, beans, and chiles. She listened to everything the Woman said and did as she was told. She didn't put her fingers in her eyes once after working with the chiles.

After dinner, the Señorita said, "I would like to make you breakfast in the morning, Señora, to show you my appreciation for all you have taught me."

"It has to be early," the Woman said. "We have much to do before the men return tomorrow."

"I will be up before you," the Señorita said. "Before the sun."

"Hmph," the Woman said. She knew the Señorita would never get up before she did. Still, if she did manage to get up and make her breakfast, how could the Woman convince her son that the Señorita would never survive out here? He needed to find another woman, someone more appropriate. The Woman heard the front door open. The Señorita must have gone out to the porch. The Woman hurried into the kitchen and got the bowl filled with the cactus thorns. She went into the Señorita's room, lifted the covering over her mattress, and sprinkled the cactus thorns over the mattress. This way, even if the owl, javelinas, and coyotes didn't keep her awake, the thorns would. She dropped the cover back down, hesitated, then left the room.

The Señorita stepped off the porch into the desert. It was a warm night and the moon was up. The owl started asking, "Who, who, who?" The Señorita knew—now—that it would fly away soon, to go hunting, and return in the morning. If she could learn the habits of an owl in only three days, what else could she learn? Her mother and grandmother had urged her to come out here, to find her roots. Look for magic.

She sighed and waved at the moon.

"Hello," she said softly. "I know I'm new to this place and I don't understand much. I do know I love a man, and his mother isn't quite sure I'm up to living out here. I'm not sure either, but I'd like a fair chance. I'm new at this. I guess I said that, didn't I? I need to get a good night's sleep, so I can wake up early. I wonder if you all could help me? I seem to have trouble sleeping with the noise—with the music—of the night. Coyotes, could you maybe croon me a lullaby? And javelinas, could you dig and snort somewhere away from the house? And anything else anyone can do to help me sleep—and wake up early—I'd really appreciate it. *Gracias!*"

The Señorita went to sleep. The Woman waited for her to cry out again, but she heard nothing. In fact, the sound of the coyotes seemed more distant tonight, or toned down. Something different. She stood by the window and waited for the javelinas, but they didn't come. And the owl must have already left to go hunting. The desert was strangely quiet.

The Señorita had the best sleep of her life. She awakened just before the sun came out when something pricked her foot. She reached down and found a single tiny thorn sticking out of the blanket.

"Thank you," she said as she got out of bed and got dressed. She dropped the thorn into the empty bowl that had been filled with thorns only the day before; then she went out into the morning to collect eggs.

The Woman got out of bed, put on her clothes, and went into the kitchen. The Señorita stood at the table, waiting. Steam rose from plates of blue corn tortillas, fried potatoes, beans, and eggs.

"*Buenos dias,* Señora," the Señorita said.

"Good day," she said as she sat at the table. The Señorita sat with her. "How did you sleep?"

"Very well," the young woman said. "I don't think I would have awakened on time except a thorn pricked me.

We must have missed one when we pulled them out the other day." She laughed.

The Woman began eating. The food was delicious!

The Woman pushed away from the table. What mischief was this? She hurried to the girl's room and lifted up the cover over the mattress. Where she had sprinkled thorns now lay feathers: all different colors and sizes of feathers.

The Woman dropped the cover and nodded. It was a good trick. A true one. To survive in the desert one needed magic. How could she have forgotten that?

The Woman Who Lived in the House returned to the kitchen and sat at the table with her future daughter-in-law.

"After breakfast, I'll show you my linens," the Woman said, "and you can pick which ones you'd like to use at the wedding."

"Thank you, Señora," she said. "That is most generous."

"You may call me Mama," the Woman said.

"Tell me, Mama," the Señorita said. "How did you end up here?"

"Ahhh," she said. "Now that is a story. It all started in the wash. Can you sing?"

"A little," the Señorita said.

"Well, wait and see," the Woman said. "I have a chorus or two I can teach you."

*—for Mario*

   

I wrote this story the first year Mario and I spent in Tucson for our winter writing retreat. I kept getting pricked by the cacti that surrounded our casita. Every time I took a walk, it seemed, I brought thorns back into the house. At night, I'd get pricked. Somehow the thorns had gotten into our bed. Mario wasn't having any trouble, but I was. I felt like the desert was giving me some kind of message. I didn't know what it was, but it inspired this story. I wrote it and left it there for Terri Windling. She read it and bought it for *Coyote Road*. I love that the Señora and the Señorita become friends in the end. I like that much better than having the stepmother or the mother-in-law trying to kill the girl!

# The Raven Sisters

Everyone knew the Raven sisters. They came from a long line of wise women and men. When the Raven sisters went into the desert—by wing or by foot—they did not want any kind of company. What they did in the desert was a mystery; it was part of the cycle of the place. The Raven sisters helped keep the world in balance.

One Raven sister was so old or so young that her feathers and hair were completely white. Her magic came from the Sun and the Stars. One Raven sister was so old or so young that her feathers and hair were the darkest blue-black anyone had ever seen. Her magic came from the Moon and the Earth.

When the air was dry enough and the wind still enough, the sisters started their annual trek into the desert.

No one ever dared to follow them.

No one except Coyote.

On this particular year, Coyote was bored, hot, and lonely. None of the women would dance with him. None of the men would hunt with him. He decided to find out what the sisters did; then everyone would want to know what he saw and what he learned.

The sisters travelled until the desert undulated in the heat, as though it would disappear into a mirage at any second. They stopped and perched on a ridge of redrock.

The sisters looked down at the empty riverbed below and the mesas beyond and prepared themselves. They fasted and sang songs. Every once in a while, a breeze fluttered their feathers. When they felt the world and their vision shift, they began.

"See that scrawny-looking tree on the redrock ridge to the north?" White Sister asked. "Let's race to it."

"Agreed," Black Sister said.

Black Sister opened her eyes wide, then jerked or coughed or shifted time, and her black eyes popped out onto the ground. White Sister did the same, and her blue eyes popped out onto the ground. The four eyes shot up and away and flew straight to the scrawny-looking tree beyond.

Coyote bit his tongue to keep from gasping in surprise.

A few moments later, the eyes flew back, so fast it seemed they were bees or tiny hummingbirds. They whizzed right into their eye sockets. Black eyes in Black Sister; blue eyes in White Sister.

"That was quite the ride." White Sister laughed. "Again?"

"Let us race to the stream below the east mesa," Black Sister said.

"Agreed."

Plop, plop. Plop, plop. Out came the eyes. They zoomed out of sight. The sisters giggled softly to themselves. A minute later, Coyote heard the whirr or whizz or whatever sound it was that meant the eyes were coming back. Slurp! Into the eye sockets they went.

"That water was refreshing," Black Sister said. "I believe I was first."

"You were," White Sister said. "I will send mine to South mountain and you to West mountains, then we will trade."

"Brilliant," Black Sister said.

Plop, plop. Plop, plop.

The eyes whipped away. The sisters stood on the ledge, nearly silent, nearly still.

A few minutes later, the eyes returned. This time the blue eyes went to Black Sister and the black eyes went to White Sister.

"Ah, this is a vision," White Sister said. "This is the way of the world."

Black Sister nodded. "Indeed."

The sisters continued racing their eyes all morning and all afternoon. They laughed, told jokes, and whispered into the wind. Finally, Coyote could stand it no longer. He burst up onto the ledge.

"Sisters," Coyote said, "I have watched you all morning and all afternoon. Please teach me this great magic."

"Coyote," White Sister said, "this is not your magic."

"You are having so much fun," he said. "I must see what you see."

"No," Black Sister said. "This isn't your vision. This is our journey."

Coyote was nothing if not persistent. He kept asking the sisters. His whining got so annoying they flew away to the next ridge. Coyote followed. By the morning, the sisters had had enough.

"If we show you how to do this, will you leave us?" Black Sister asked.

"I will, I promise!"

The sisters looked at one another.

"All right," White Sister said. "Lay down. This is going to hurt, but you cannot move no matter what."

"No matter what."

Coyote sprawled on the rocky ground. He looked up at the two sisters and smiled. Then he felt searing pain and everything went black.

Each sister plucked out one of Coyote's eyes and swallowed it.

It had been many days since they had eaten.

"Yum," Black Sister said.

"Yummy," White Sister said.

They flew away.

Coyote waited on the ledge for his eyes to return.

After a time, Coyote figured his eyes had gotten lost on their way back to him. He carefully climbed down the ledge and walked around the desert. He could hardly wait to see what his eyes had seen.

"Come home, little eyes," he yipped.

Since Coyote could not see, he walked into too many cacti and nearly stepped on one too many rattlesnakes. One day he felt something slippery, round, and cool beneath his feet.

"My eyes!" he cried. "I have found you!"

He picked up one and then the other and pushed them into his eye sockets.

He blinked and shook his head. He looked around and saw light. He saw the yellow cranberries on the ground all around him. He saw clouds in the blue sky. The world appeared a bit different than it had before. He was certain this was because his eyes had seen many great things.

Coyote howled his delight and began the trek home.

And that is how the Raven Sisters continued to keep balance in the world without Coyote tagging along and how Coyote's eyes went from black to yellow.

Coyote never did tell the story of the racing eyes to anyone else. He figured some visions were for Coyote alone.

◆◆◆

This is based on a Native American story that is often called "The Eye Juggler." I've seen many versions of the story. Most sources say it's a Cheyenne story, although it's also part of Ji-carilla Apache folklore, as far as I can tell. Like most Coyote sto-ries, it is universal. And something about this story just makes me giggle no matter what version I hear.

# A Strange Attractor

I dreamed I was on my momma's front porch. She and Aunt Sue danced, their feet bending the old gray boards, their hands shaking their skirts. They danced to the tune of the swamp beyond. I drank the air as they danced, drank the moisture the swamp had sent us.

"Why do you dance?" I asked Momma.

"I dance for our sisters in Africa," she told me, "so they will have the fortune of our water."

"I dance for our sister up North," Aunt Sue said, "whose ass is so tight, she's been full of shit for years."

Then they both laughed so hard their feet stopped moving and only their bellies danced. Momma leaned down and kissed my mouth.

I awakened gulping the air. But I tasted no moisture. Louisiana was a world away. And I was tired.

My cot creaked as I slowly sat up and ran my fingers through my dusty black hair. I needed to cut it. Here, so close to the ever expanding Sahara, my hair had become almost straight. Ironic how I came to the Africa of my great great grandparents only to have my French ancestry rear its ugly white head. My skin couldn't take the sun, so I had to keep my body covered. I was paler than most of the few white people in town. Fortunately, I had stopped bringing out photos of my great grandparents to prove I was a true African. Nobody cared.

"Bethany, get your sweet butt out of bed. We're burning daylight. I don't know how you can sleep through those guinea fowl crowing before dawn anyway."

"Good morning to you, too, John. And I don't sleep through it, I just fall back to sleep after they've finished."

John opened the white curtain that separated my sleeping space from the rest of the mud house we shared. On our rickety kitchen table I could see steam rising. Breakfast.

"We've got some big shot coming in from Egypt today," he said.

"I didn't know there were big shots in drought research."

I grabbed a pair of pants and pulled them on, then went into the other room. I had come to Africa as John's assistant, on sabbatical from my teaching job, yet John seemed to do more for me than I for him. He had stepped off the plane and been hit with a kind of indomitable energy; I had come down with a case of ennui that would not quit.

I sat at the table and stared at my plate of food for a moment. Rice and peanut sauce. It seemed as though I had eaten this every day for weeks.

"What would you like me to do today?" I asked as I picked up my spoon.

"Something to get you out of this funk."

He smiled, and I stuck out my tongue at him. We had been friends since we were kids, growing up in the same neighborhood in New Orleans. Well, not the same, exactly. He liked to come to my house and see what the voodoo sisters were up to. I liked to go to his house and look at the matching furniture and the white sofas and chintz curtains. I liked the smells in our house better. His house smelled of cinnamon. Mine of cayenne. Or hot peppers. A combination of hot and spicy, with fragrances from the marsh, too, mixing it all into a heady brew.

"Why don't you just walk around town today, get to know the place."

"John! I don't speak any of the languages. And I never know what I'll do wrong."

He laughed.

"Hey, I'm a woman in a predominantly Muslim country."

"Get over it, Oya-goya!" he said. "Nobody cares. These people are just trying to get from one day to the next. They don't even know you're here. You are exceedingly paranoid."

He shoveled the last bit of rice into his mouth and then pushed his chair away from the table.

"Okay. I'll reform," I said. "I'll try to be cheerful. I'll go to work with you and be the belle of the ball."

"Does that mean I can call you by your real name, *Oya*?"

"My real name is Bethany. I'll show you my birth certificate."

He rolled his eyes. We went outside into the bright sunshine. The sky hung over us, pale blue, extending forever. Our square mud house, a gift from the local chieftain, stood against others, some the same, others wooden with tin roofs. We hurried toward our office, down the dusty path past donkeys, brightly dressed women carrying baskets to the weekly market, men in white dress talking together, and children chasing the guinea fowl. I tried, as I tried every day, to take in the sights and smells, but my system was on overload. My eyes glazed over at the foreignness of it all until I saw very little. Gold dust hung everywhere, almost incarnate, following everything and everyone as a reminder, "I am the Sahara, and I am coming." When I closed my eyes at night, the blue sky was an after-image on my brain.

I had traveled easily during my life before coming to Mali, exploring the US, Canada, Mexico, Western Europe. I had always felt excited by the new and strange. But here. Here, I swallowed dust and longed to wallow in the swamps of home. Here, I went by my Christian name instead of Oya, a kind of hubris on my mother's part to call her daughter after an African goddess. Or after a river, tornado, lightning, manner of dress. Depending upon who was telling the story. Here, I felt far from myself and home.

"We all come from Africa," Momma often told me, "no matter how white or how black we are. Africa is home to the human race."

Well then, Thomas Wolfe was right. You can't go home again.

Our office was in a part of town left over from French rule. The building resembled a piece of Europe plucked down in the middle of the desert, unlike the rest of this village south of Timbouctou which seemed more Arabian than African to me. We liked our office building for many reasons, but mostly because it had indoor plumbing. Today, John and I raced into this anachronism to see who would get to the toilet first.

"Hah!" John said when we reached the closed door to the sacred bathroom. "This is your fault for getting up late."

"You're such a baby." I laughed and left him to wait and went into our office. Several team members were already there looking over data, sitting at the computer, or drinking coffee. Out of the six of them, half were black, half white, and then me, of course. John and I were the only Americans.

Billie looked up at me. "Hello, Beth," she said in her clipped British accent. She was Nigerian, educated at Oxford. "We've gotten more casualty figures." She shook her head. "As goes Africa, so goes the world."

I sat in one of the unsteady chairs. Maybe that's why I had so little energy. Every day we were faced with what seemed like the end of the world: disease, drought, war, and famine were ravaging Africa. Every day brought another prediction of worldwide catastrophe. No, that wasn't right: Every day brought confirmation that the world was in the midst of the apocalypse.

The big shot from Egypt gave a lecture about deforestation. People from all around the region attended. I daydreamed most of the time, hearing enough to know I had heard it before. Deforestation was causing the drought. Without trees, there was no humidity. Without humidity, or mountains, or something to dance with, the wind just caused havoc, eating up everything in its path.

Including the people. The wind and sun parched their souls.

"O-ya, O-ya, she rips, she tears it."

I opened my eyes and looked around the conference room. Everyone was standing and talking to one another.

Who had said my name?

I looked across the room and caught the gaze of one of the few women there. She had the most beautiful blue-black skin. She smiled at me, then turned away.

"Well, there's our solution," John said, coming up behind me. "We'll just plant trees and everything will be fine. Or maybe it's really the livestock. We'll shoot them all. Or maybe we need more livestock. We'll import some. Then we'll fix the ozone layer and stop the greenhouse effect. Then there's stopping the wars." He laughed. "Ain't life simple?"

I patted him on the back. I knew how he felt. It was difficult for us to study it, to see the devastating effects and not know what to do to help. We all wanted to do something. *I* wanted to do something.

But I felt annihilated by the enormity of it all.

I sighed. I longed for the relative safety of the hallowed halls of the University of Chicago, where I had fled Louisiana and my family to teach literature and live an uncomplicated life. Where the wind sheered off Lake Michigan straight into a wall of skyscrapers.

"O-ya. O-ya."

I looked across the room again, but the woman was gone.


Today was market day; on the way home, John and I walked through the marketplace. It was filled mostly with women of all hues, colors, and costumes, each selling her own wares: oil, maize, millet, rice, peanuts, occasional jewelry, cloth, prepared food. Some sat on blankets on the ground, others had put together tiny portable shops to display their goods. I followed John, half-conscious that the sun was starting to slide away. Shadows fell from the various rickety structures, looking like tossed off clothing. I stopped to buy peanuts while John wandered ahead of me. The seller's face was gaunt, her gaze blank as she took my money. I opened the paper around the peanuts, began shelling them, and popped the naked beans into my mouth.

I had heard that the marketplace was a place of freedom for women here. A kind of room of their own. Amazing what a little commerce could do for one's sense of freedom. I breathed the dust and a bit of cool air and stood in the near dusk looking around. The babble of languages was a quiet lullaby. For a moment, things seemed normal, familiar. The rhythm of life maintained despite the drought.

On the periphery of my vision, I saw a flash of white. Without thinking, I moved toward the white. On the edges of the market, in the shadow of a hut, an old wrinkled woman danced, her eyes closed, her bare feet moving slowly in the dust. "O-ya, O-ya," she murmured, her fingers signing some unknowable message to the air.

"She's like the wind, lost without the water. Imploding. Exploding. Creativity without outlet."

I turned around. The woman from the conference stood there, dressed in shiny blue cloth.

"I am Nyalé," she said, holding out a hand to me. I gently shook it.

"I'm—"

"Oya," she answered.

"Bethany," I said.

"Ahhh. So you aren't Oya the goddess of the marketplace?"

I laughed. "She's that, too? And about a hundred other

   

things. Okay, you caught me, my mother does call me Oya, though I don't know how you knew that. But I thought I should stick to Bethany while I was here. Do you know this woman?" I turned to the old woman, but she was gone.

"Hundreds of years ago, she would have been honored," Nyalé said, "probably a healer of some kind, or a psychic. Now she is one of the powerful seen as powerless."

"*Seen* as powerless? You mean she *is* powerful?"

She shrugged. We began walking through the market. The women were loading their unsold goods into baskets; their journeys home would soon begin.

"Are you part of the commission?" I asked.

Nyalé shook her head. "No, I'm just visiting for a while. It's good to talk in English with you. It's not often I can practice here. Would you like to have lunch with me to-morrow?"

"Sure," I answered, surprised and unexpectedly pleased.

"I'll meet you at your office then," she said.

We had reached the end of the market.

"That'll be great," I said.

"There you are," John said, suddenly behind me. "I thought you'd gotten lost."

"Not me. I just met this nice woman." I turned back to Nyalé, but she was gone again, dusk now marking the trodden path leading away from the market. "Well, she was just here. It was nice to talk about something besides the drought."

"Oh? What'd you talk about?"

"Crazy old women." I laughed and took his arm. "Let's go home. I'm hungry!"

Nyalé waited outside for me the next day at lunch time. I brought some of the foodstuffs the Egyptian had left as presents for us, including rice wrapped in grape leaves and bottled water. We walked beside each other toward the Niger. When we got to it, we stopped above the river which uncoiled before us like a continent-sized cobra, sunning itself across a fair portion of West Africa. Grass grew here, along with several trees. Long boats floated in the shallow water near the shore, their ends curled up like the shoes of a giant genie. We joined others under a shade tree, women and children, relaxed and talkative, the sun and desert shaded from their eyes. Across the Niger, the desert waited.

"The Djoliba—the Niger—used to flood during the rainy season," Nyalé said as we sat beside each other, "bringing nourishment to many villages along her path. Now, she hardly floods at all. It's as though she's forgotten how."

Above us, a bright blue parrot-like bird called out. I waved to it. Nyalé smiled.

"Do you think she can do it?" Nyalé asked.

"She who? And what?" I handed her the box of grape leaves.

"Can the river keep the desert at bay?"

I stared across the water at the Sahara. I breathed deeply, taking in a touch of moisture, a mouthful of dust. I shook my head. "No."

Nyalé laughed. "So little faith."

"I've seen the facts."

"Ah yes, the facts. I heard the man from Egypt yesterday, too. Some say the drought is caused by the socioeconomic problems of the area. Colonialism, Islam, it all took away our religions and women's power. Hundreds of years without truly free women's mysteries have created this." She waved her hand toward the desert. "Others say it is because most of the people worship Allah, or Jehovah: They are desert gods, so a desert is what they get!"

"Things seem so complicated here," I said. "I came to Africa hoping for a little primal simplicity. What a joke! The more I learn, the more confused I am. So many different beliefs, religions, goddesses, gods, governments, ways of looking at things. Even Oya, my namesake, she's either a goddess, a wife, a force of nature, or a whirlwind of cloth to banish disease."

"That seems complicated to you? Maybe she is all those things. Or different aspects to different people. Just as you are different to different people."

I bit off part of a grape leaf. "A piece of cloth *and* a goddess? I think I'm pretty much the same wherever I am."

I thought of my mother and Aunt Sue dancing on our porch. They could be explosively happy one moment and foretelling the end of the world the next. Dancing on the porch through it all. They had always wanted me to dance with them, but I wouldn't. Too shy, they said. But that hadn't been it. I hadn't known how to dance and was afraid I'd misstep.

Seemed ridiculous now. I should have danced with them—danced until the rains fell on our sisters in Africa, or loosened up my aunt in the North who happened to look and act a lot like me.

I smiled. Nyalé handed me the water.

"Funny, you say you're always the same," Nyalé said. "I've seen you around the village. Sometimes I look at you, and you seem as black and African as I am. Other times you are very fair-skinned, very European. I have seen a vase like that: one side the face of a black woman, the other side a white woman."

"That's me. Voodoo or Catholic. Black or white. Tight-assed or loose."

"*Or*? Can't you be Voudon *and* Catholic, black *and* white? Many different things. Like Oya."

We ate in silence for a time. Then we talked of my family and home. After we finished, we returned to town and shook hands at my office.

"Tomorrow they are dancing at the river. Would you like to come and watch? The water-spirit priest said I could invite you."

"As long as I don't have to dance, I'd love to come."

Nyalé shook her head and smiled. "You never know what will happen when you take a chance. See you at dawn then." She waved good-bye.

The news was not good. More satellite pictures. More meteorological data. More death and starvation. I felt frozen in place as John recited one statistic after another.

"As goes Africa, so goes the world."

I suddenly envisioned the Earth encased in sand. No moisture in sight. The wind whipping up one catastrophe after another.

"O-ya, O-ya."

Like the woman in the marketplace. Nowhere to go. No one to dance with. Imploding. Exploding. Nothing to do but watch it happen.

John was still sleeping in his part of the house when I got up. I put on a long red wrinkled skirt and blouse and went into the dawn. The sky was rose-colored, the buildings pink and gold. Nyalé, wrapped in shiny royal purple cloth, waited for me. She took my hand, and we hurried toward the festivities. I laughed as she pulled me along the dirt path. I felt like a girl again, running past the dawn-colored one-story buildings and the brightly dressed villagers straggling toward the river. Long canoes rocked gently in the black water. Across the wide river, turban-headed men swayed gently atop saddled camels.

Chaos ruled the event. Or so it seemed. Music began. I heard bata drums somewhere. Or was it the sound of water over rocks. Snakes across earth? I squatted on the ground, legs open beneath my skirt, rocking. The dancers began while the water-spirit priests watched. The dancers—male or female, I could not tell which—wore costumes with colors so vibrant only nature could have created them. Their feet moved to music I could not hear, their hands making shapes I did not understand, each doing their own dance.

"The river speaks," Nyalé told me. "She is a storyteller, the Djoliba, Oya's river. The dancers are remembering as the river remembers. Or, as some believe, they are actually helping the Djoliba to remember."

"My mom used to dance for her sisters in Africa," I said. "Her great great grandparents were Yoruba. She said the dance was to help bless them with water. Do these dancers study a long time to learn the steps?"

Nyalé laughed. "They did not go to school to learn this dance. They are dancing as the element of water in their bodies dances—we are mostly water, remember. The element of water in them shows them how to dance."

The land ached for water, I thought. Could nature have forgotten how to make water? Just as the river had forgotten to flood? What we needed was some kind of force of nature.

Perhaps that was what the old woman in the market had been doing: dancing up a storm. O-ya, O-ya. Force of nature.

After the dancing, chaos reigned again, yet coalesced into a kind of sense. I thought I saw the old woman once, but when I looked again, it was only Nyalé bringing me tea. I ate millet and rice and peanut sauce and sucked on a kola nut. Everyone seemed in good spirits; some even spoke French to me, believing, I suppose, that I could speak it, too. I smiled and nodded, though I didn't understand much more than a few words.

"This was wonderful," I said to Nyalé. "To have a celebration in the middle of a drought is so odd and wonderful."

"What better time!"

"Of course you are right. You can have joy and sadness. That's always been difficult for me to understand. I've always wanted a line to delineate good from bad, happiness from unhappiness. I want things to be simple."

"Perhaps things are more simple than you think," Nyalé said.

I shook my head. "One thing that I've learned is that there are no simple answers to anything."

"Perhaps the simple answer is that all the answers are right."

"Or wrong," I said.

"Have you heard that one butterfly flapping its wings in Australia can cause a monsoon in Japan?"

"Really? Well, finally, the solution to our problems! We need to get a whole bunch of butterflies flapping their wings to cause it to rain here!" I laughed.

"Oya. I said *one* butterfly. Just one."


That night, I dreamed I saw a group of women chanting and dancing in a circle. I decided I couldn't join them, but one woman called me forward. As soon as they linked hands with me, the circle disintegrated. Then the world was coming to a cataclysmic end: thunder, lightning, earthquakes. I was in a huge room with hundreds of people. I said we should all hold hands and dance. That would save the world. Of course I couldn't get them all to dance, and

I was certain now all would end, but I kept dancing any-way and soon the apocalypse stopped. It had worked even though I hadn't done it right. The world was saved.

I awakened to the guinea fowl trumpeting the coming of dawn. I got dressed and walked toward the river. The sky was rose-colored. The river was a snake, waiting, sleeping?

As I got closer to the shore, where the long boats sat empty, I saw a figure dancing. Nyalé. I waved and hurried toward her, eager to tell her my dream. As I got closer, I realized it was the old woman from the marketplace. Her feet and hands danced, her white-hair bobbed up and down, her eyes were closed.

"O-ya, O-ya," she said, opening her eyes when I was a few feet from her.

She held a hand out to me.

I smiled. I could not plant all the trees, or empower all the women, or change the way people worshiped. I could not stop the wars. But maybe I could remember how to dance.

I held the woman's hand and stepped into her circle. She took her hand back, closed her eyes and danced her chaos. I kicked off my shoes and dug my toes into the earth and started to dance. My feet and hands moved to some song only the river and air knew.

"We dance for our sisters." Nyalé's voice. I opened my eyes; the old woman's eyes were still closed, and she was lost in her dance. I breathed deeply as the element of water within me danced. For a moment, I thought I gulped a bit of Louisiana air, moist and sweet. I could almost hear the porch boards squeaking as my mother and her sister danced.

"O-ya, O-ya," Nyalé chanted.

I tasted the beads of sweat on my upper lip.

I was creating water.

I laughed.

Like the butterfly, I was a force of nature.

♦♦♦

This story came from my own social and environmental activism. Often I feel as though I can't accomplish anything because it's all too big. At the time I wrote this story, I was reading any book on any goddess, and I had just read Judith Gleason's fascinating *Oya: In Praise of an African Goddess*. So much of it was like reading Greek to me. I couldn't understand how this goddess could be a force of nature and a piece of cloth, a goddess and a wife. Finally I had to get my logical mind out of the way and just go with it—go with her. Dance with her. And so "A Strange Attractor" was born.

Kim Antieau has written many novels, short stories, poems, and essays. Her work has appeared in numerous publications, both in print and online, including *The Magazine of Fantasy and Science Fiction, Asimov's SF, The Clinton Street Quarterly, The Journal of Mythic Arts, EarthFirst!, Alternet, Sage Woman,* and *Alfred Hitchcock's Mystery Magazine.* She was the founder, editor, and publisher of *Daughters of Nyx: A Magazine of Goddess Stories, Mythmaking, and Fairy Tales.* Her work has twice been shortlisted for the James Tiptree Award and has appeared in many best-of-the-year anthologies. Critics have admired her "literary fearlessness" and her vivid language and imagination. Her first novel, *The Jigsaw Woman,* is a modern classic of feminist literature. She is also the author of a science fiction novel, *The Gaia Websters,* and a contemporary tale set in the desert Southwest, *Church of the Old Mermaids.* Her other novels include *Her Frozen Wild, The Fish Wife,* and *Coyote Cowgirl. Broken Moon,* a novel for young adults, was a selection of the Junior Library Guild. She has also written other YA novels, including *Deathmark, The Blue Tail, Ruby's Imagine,* and *Mercy, Unbound.* Kim lives in the Pacific Northwest with her husband, writer Mario Milosevic. Learn more about Kim and her writing at www.kimantieau.com.

www.ingramcontent.com/pod-product-compliance
Lightning Source LLC
Chambersburg PA
CBHW032047180726
48284CB00004B/1223